VIKING'S CLAIM

CALLED BY A VIKING
BOOK TWO

MARIAH STONE

GET A FREE MARIAH STONE BOOK!

Join Mariah's mailing list to be the first to know of new releases, free books, special prices, and other author giveaways.

freehistoricalromancebooks.com

Also by Mariah Stone

Mariah's Time Travel Romance Series

- Called by a Highlander
- Called by a Viking
- Called by a Pirate
- Fated

Mariah's Regency Romance Series

- Dukes and Secrets

View All of Mariah's Books in Reading Order

Scan the QR code for the complete list of Mariah's ebooks, paperbacks, and audiobooks in reading order.

Power to the tall girls.

PROLOGUE

Hvaldalen, Norway, September 30, 875 AD

Andor Thornsson stared at the gray cloud of smoke right above his village.

"It is on fire," Fridstein said.

"I have eyes in my face, Fridstein, not on my arse," Andor said to his second-in-command through gritted teeth.

They both stood on the bow of the longship, which cut through the water towards home, a small village at the end of the fjord huddled in a green valley between looming mountains. Andor's eyes hurt from straining to see through the smoke, and his stomach sank further as it became clear that no one moved in the village.

Silence hung over the ship.

The sickening scent of burning wood, flesh and hair filled Andor's nostrils and he gripped the side of the dragon figurehead. Drizzle fell in a fine mist, so the wood of the houses was likely wet, and the fire might be nearly out or dying. Perhaps it was not too late to save his people.

"Faster!" Andor yelled to his rowing men without turning. His command would be passed to the two other ships that followed him home. "Hurry, you Loki's sons. Your wives and children might be burning."

Andor's own wife, Svana, might be, too. Terror scraped at his heart.

The ship cut the still waters quicker, his men grunting as one every time the oars sank into the water.

"Can you see anyone, Jarl?" Fridstein said.

"No," he said, fear gripping his gut and turning his blood to ashes. "Be ready to kill anyone who is not ours." He unsheathed Dragon's Trouble, the sword Svana had given him as a wedding present a year ago.

His green-eyed, brown-haired, beautiful wife...Svana had to be all right. She had to be, Odin. If she was not...

He would never forgive himself.

"Faster!" he cried.

The ship crawled, even though the oars rose and fell faster than Andor thought was humanly possible. But the closer they got, the more the charcoal frames of the buildings protruded from the gray wall of smoke. And the tighter his stomach coiled.

The ship barely touched the jetty, and Andor and his men jumped onto the wooden surface, shields, swords, and axes at the ready. A body lay on the quay—the shepherd.

"Thor's sweaty arse," Andor spat.

"Protect the jarl," Fridstein cried behind him, and Andor knew his loyal band followed. He gestured, and his men advanced without taking cover; they were swift but alert.

Around the village, people Andor had known his whole life lay dead and injured. Cows, sheep, and goats were slaughtered.

Rye, parsnips, herbs, and other food was scattered on the ground. Most houses stood burned, some more than others. There was no fire anymore, just smoke.

His heart sank when he saw the biggest source of smoke—his mead hall.

His home.

"Svana!" Andor called.

Screams of pain rang out across the village. His men who were closest to the houses and the bushes were fighting and falling with their throats cut. Warriors poured from behind corners, their eyes drunk with violence, their swords and axes atilt. His men launched at them, and the air filled with cries, the clinking of metal, and the thumping of wood.

"Kill the bastards!" Andor yelled.

Battle fury raged in his veins, but cold fear stabbed his gut. Where was Svana? If any of them as much as touched one hair on her head—

He needed to find her—now.

He dodged the first man's ax and pierced him in the side, between the chest and back plates of his leather armor. The next one almost got him, but Andor whirled and cut his neck. Then he saw her. The edge of her favorite cornflower-blue linen dress showed just behind the corner of the blackened walls of his longhouse. His heart thumped, his limbs chilling. He darted there, slashing, kicking, piercing anyone in his way.

"Protect the jarl!" Fridstein's voice called out behind him, and he knew his men had his back.

When he finally reached the longhouse, he found her on the wet ground, a gaping wound in her side.

"Svana!" Andor sank to his knees by her side, the battle be damned.

He knew Fridstein and his men were fighting off anyone who would consider attacking him and his wounded wife.

Andor scooped Svana into his arms and held her close. Her lashes fluttered, and she opened her eyes. They fixed on him, and she smiled. "Andor."

"Do not speak," he said. "Kall is here, he will cure you."

She shook her head. "Freya's Valkyries are already waiting to take me to Fólkvangr. I am glad she let me see you before I go."

Andor squeezed her tight to his chest. "No. I will not let her take you."

"Why were you late?" she whispered. "You promised to be back to me a moon ago. Are you whole?"

Andor's eyes burned, his muscles as tense as ropes. Guilt gripped him and smashed him like a boulder. The wound looked bad, but he was not going to let her die.

"Kall!" he cried for the healer. "Here!"

He turned back to her, his chest aching.

"I am whole. I was late because Ubba—"

He was late because Ubba Ragnarsson had asked him to raid a monastery in Wessex and bring him a Bible the Saxons valued more than gold. He'd rewarded him with land, silver, and treasure. Andor told himself he'd done all that for Svana, but Jarl Andor Thornsson was now famous in all the Norse lands and in Bretland. Which was the real reason he'd broken his word to the woman he loved.

Why was he thinking about land, treasure, and silver? He should be saying how much he loved her.

"It does not matter why I was late, my love," he said. "I brought us riches and fame. But I should never have let you get hurt. If only I had come when I promised..."

Svana shook her head. "I am proud of you, my husband." She touched his cheek.

Guilt gripped Andor's throat. Svana had been everything he had hoped for in a wife. She loved him, she kept the household in excellent order, and her word was cast-iron. Pride for her, love for her, filled every part of him with warmth.

"Kall! Heal her!" He bellowed, but his voice was lost in the noise of the battle.

Svana swallowed. She was as pale as cotton grass, and her eyes closed. "I must let go now, Andor. I wanted to be a good wife to you..." she whispered.

And froze.

She lay motionless in his arms. Her chest did not rise any longer.

A gentle breeze brought smoke from the remnants of Andor's house, and it singed his eyes and throat.

He pressed his wife against his chest, burying his face in her silky hair, inhaling her scent mixed with the iron tang of blood. "I should have been here," he whispered into her ear. "I should have protected you."

He took her hand in his, the hand that had caressed him, the hand that he had hoped would soothe their future children. The hand that would, one day, have waved goodbye to him, old and gray, on the way to his final battle. Andor kissed her still-warm forehead. Shame scorched his neck and face like the coals that were all that remained of the village he had failed to protect.

"I am sorry, Svana," he whispered against her soft skin. The Valkyries would hear his words and carry them to her spirit. "You were everything a man could hope for in a wife. None can replace you. None ever will."

He held her for a moment longer, then used his arm to sweep the tears from his face and beard. With guilt as heavy as a granite torc around his neck, he rose, the desire for vengeance sucking at his lungs, drying his mouth, making his bones ache.

"Who did this?" he roared. "Who killed my wife?"

Fridstein delivered a deadly strike to an enemy warrior. "It was that worm, Elgr," Fridstein threw across his shoulder, his breath heavy. "Look! He is trying to cut his way to the ships."

A predator's roar shot up Andor's throat and reverberated in his whole body. All his men fought the intruders and the ships were unguarded, there for the taking. If Elgr put just ten men on each ship, they could sail away with everything.

Andor would have given all of his treasure and all of his ships for a chance to save Svana's life. But it was too late for that. Elgr had already taken everything he truly cared about.

The need for revenge, for the blood of his enemies, intensified to a fever pitch within him. He threw himself back into the battle, pursuing Elgr. But no cut, no thrust, no life he took brought him relief.

Finally, he closed in on the other jarl. The man was his age and their lands bordered each other, but they had never been friends. Elgr had always seemed envious of whatever Andor had, from his fierce warriors to his hearty crops to his beautiful wife.

"Come here, you worm!" Andor roared, pointing his sword in Elgr's face. "Fight me. You will pay for her death." Elgr was as tall as Andor but soft around the middle, while Andor was a fighter, honed from months of battle. There would be no contest in a fair fight—something Elgr knew little about.

"Pay for her death?" Elgr glanced at Andor, jostled the man he was fighting off and made his way to him, hunger for Andor's death in his eyes. "She just paid for being your wife."

Elgr thrust his sword towards Andor, and Andor deflected it. "Ubba always gave me the best raids until you came along," Elgr yelled. Another thrust. "He should have given me the task to get the Bible." *Clunk.* "This silver and treasure are mine."

Andor roared and attacked, hammering at Elgr's shield with Dragon's Trouble. "You. Pig. Loki's. Son."

His rage burned him, the sight of Svana's dying face, her voice ringing louder than the battle around him.

"You. Will. Pay." His words knocked against the shield with each bash.

He took his ax out and, with his other hand, slammed it into the shield and split the wood. The ax stuck, and he jerked hard, sending the shield flying to the side.

"This is for burning my village," Andor roared and thrust Dragon's Trouble into Elgr's stomach. He pulled back and stabbed him again. "That was for my people." Elgr fell to his knees clutching at his stomach, and Andor swung his sword and cut the man's head off. "And that was for Svana."

As the battle continued to whirl, bang, and burst in screams around him, he stood still, his chest rising and falling heavily, his muscles still tight with fury. He had his vengeance.

But what now? He did not feel satisfied. He had not been redeemed.

It had not brought Svana back.

Nothing ever would.

Her voice rang in his ears. "Why were you late...? Are you whole...? I wanted to be a good wife to you..." The screams of unprotected women and children from the village joined Svana's voice. Then the clunking of weapons. Andor's fists clenched. Panic, guilt, and the pain of loss all mixed within him like a whirlpool in a storm.

As Elgr's men saw the death of their leader, they began cowering, retreating, and Andor's warriors killed them or let them run.

When the battle was over and the village stood still, littered with the dead and the injured, Andor took Svana's body to the fjord. He gently laid her on the pebble beach and straightened, watching the descending, misty dusk as smoke dulled the setting sun.

"What now, Jarl?" Fridstein said, standing next to him. Andor heard the same sadness in his sword-brother's voice that tightened his own chest. "When do we start rebuilding Hvaldalen?"

Andor stared out into the distance to where the fjord disappeared. "We do not. There are too many ghosts here, too many reminders. I will go back to serve Ubba. I will take Svana's parents, give them a farm. Land there is richer and more fertile. Ubba owes me. All surviving families are welcome to come. They lost their livelihood because I failed to protect them. This is the least I can do."

Fridstein frowned. "This is not your fault, brother."

Andor lowered his head and shook it, his vision blurred, and the muscles on his cheekbones trembled. "I broke my promise. And I must pay for it."

"The best thing to do is to stay and start anew. Rebuild. Give your people back their homes. Be their jarl."

Andor let out a shaky breath. "All there is left for me is battle. I will not remain in the place that breathes with the memory of my wife."

Fridstein pressed his lips into a thin line within his beard. "Your father would have wanted you to find a new one."

He might as well have stabbed Andor in the gut. "I can never take another wife, Fridstein. Do you not see? I cannot protect the ones I love." He looked at the charred skeleton of the home he would never return to. "I will not endure this again."

CHAPTER ONE

Los Angeles, January 8, 2019

"That's better, Brad," Cathy said as she lifted the breathing tube to wipe the remaining shaving foam from her fiancé's chin. "I can see your face again."

She studied him, hoping for a twitch, a flutter of eyelashes, or any other sign. Nothing moved except for the pump of the ventilation machine next to him and the line of his heart monitor.

She forced a smile and said, "I believe in miracles. I believe you'll come back to me."

The affirmation felt increasingly fake the more times she said it, like she was lying to herself.

"You relax and rest, babe," she murmured. "When you get out of this coma, you'll be groomed and fresh, as though you just slept for a long time." She kissed him on the tip of his nose.

Then she applied his favorite aftershave. She inhaled the masculine scent of it, her mind filling with memories of watching Brad in the bathroom mirror as he slapped it on his cheeks. He inevitably grimaced as it stung him, and he made that "ohh-ahhh" sound that always made her smile.

Cathy watched closely, hoping to see an echo of the grimace.

But none came.

She put the shaving accessories in her purse, then gently picked a dark-blond lock from his shoulder. "Yeah, babe, it's time for a haircut. Tomorrow."

The edges of his hair were bleached from the sunlight he had been exposed to every day being a professional surfer and instructor, but the new hair that had grown since he'd been in the ICU was the color of dark wheat. She wished she could look into his blue eyes again. She wished she could see him smile at her. Tell her how beautiful she looked today. Tell her how much he loved her.

Tears welled in Cathy's eyes. She cupped his jaw and brushed one of his high cheekbones with her thumb. "Come back to me, Brad," she whispered. "Please come back to me."

A knock made her jump and she stood up, quickly wiping her tears, then turned around. Dr. Gentzelman and Brad's dad, Eric, stood in the doorway. Eric was Brad's double, only older. Tall, well-built, with thick, blond hair that was already graying, he had the same blue eyes and a square jaw. But during the last twelve months, his shoulders had become slouched and dark circles had appeared under his eyes. And for the first time, Cathy noticed that he had begun to look like an old man.

"Hi, Cathy," Dr. Gentzelman said. "Are we interrupting?"

Cathy pressed out a smile. "No, no. Of course not. Sorry, I'm just a bit emotional today."

Dr. Gentzelman shook her head and smiled back politely. "Don't apologize. I can't imagine how hard it must be for you." She looked at Eric and added. "For both of you."

The lines around Eric's mouth deepened.

Cathy tucked her hair behind her ear. "I was already leaving, so you can have your time with him."

She took her purse and was about to walk out when Eric said, "I need to talk to you, Cathy."

With a sinking feeling in her stomach, Cathy gave a curt nod and looked at him.

"He isn't getting better," he said. "It's been more than a year. Linda and I—we want to let him go."

Cathy closed her eyes, pain crushing, whirling, knocking her, stealing the ground under her feet.

When she opened her eyes, Dr. Gentzelman and Eric were all blurry. "No," Cathy said.

"You need to consider it, Cathy," Dr. Gentzelman said. "I'm so sorry to say this, but Brad's coma is most likely permanent. His brain shows almost no signs of activity, and after a year, the chances of him returning are almost null. We are keeping his body breathing and supplying it with nutrients, but Brad is not with us anymore."

Cathy shook her head. "You don't know that. He could still be in there. People come out of comas all the time."

"Not after a year, Cathy."

Eric's chin trembled. He was looking at the floor, but finally he raised his eyes, red and watery. "You're torturing him, Cathy. You're torturing us—all of us, yourself included. He wants to go. Let him!"

He might as well have punched her in the stomach. She stopped breathing from the pain she heard in his words.

Seeing her reaction, Eric pressed. "He should never have given you the power to decide this. We're his parents. If the legal decision was in our hands, we'd already have let him go. We're ready."

Dr. Gentzelman covered Cathy's hand with hers. "Maybe it's time you get ready, too."

Tears fell down Cathy's face. Her chest hurt. Hell, her whole body hurt. "No! While there's still hope—"

"But there isn't!" Eric yelled.

Dr. Gentzelman shook her head. "I'm so sorry."

Cathy looked back at Brad, who was lying peacefully, as though he was just asleep and would wake up and they'd go to the beach. "I do *not* accept that," she said. "If I'm the only one fighting for his life, well then so be it."

Eric sighed and pinched the bridge of his nose. "We'll give you two weeks to come to terms with letting him go, Cathy. If you don't give your permission in two weeks, we'll take legal action. I can't allow you to keep my son trapped here in this bed when I know he wants to go."

Hot waves of anger and fear hit Cathy in the face. She whirled around, bent down and kissed Brad's cheek. The after-shave mixed with his scent filled her nostrils. She stopped for a moment before Eric. "Please, hear me. I do *not* give my permission to stop his life support. Do you understand?" She turned to Dr. Gentzelman. "You are not allowed to stop those machines."

Cathy waited for Dr. Gentzelman's small nod then stormed out of the hospital room.

She made her way out of the building on autopilot, Eric's words thundering in her ears, until she came to a stop at her yellow Volkswagen New Beetle in the parking lot. Getting inside made her feel like a giant trying to fit into a porcelain cup. She would so much rather drive a Range Rover, which would fit her height and size much better. But Brad was right. Small cars saved the environment and made parking easier, and the color radiated the sun.

Radiated California.

So unlike her.

But as long as their surfboards fit, that was all they needed.

Cathy had already strapped her board to the roof rack as she'd planned on catching some waves after teaching her yoga class. But after the conversation she'd just had, yoga was the last thing on her mind. She called in sick with the studio then maneuvered out of the hospital parking lot into the surprisingly warm winter's day.

Anger and desperation whirled inside her, boiling, bashing.

She needed to be at the beach. Where everything had started. Where she'd first met Brad five years ago. Where they had planned to open a surf and yoga school. Where they were supposed to get married.

And where the people who were supposed to be his friends had driven Brad away—to his death.

Not death! He was not dead yet.

The drive to Sonada Beach crawled, and Cathy watched the familiar scene flash by—the houses, palm trees and hills she had seen countless times on the same ride with Brad. Finally, Cathy parked up the hill and quickly changed into her wetsuit. It was hot pink—Brad had chosen the color as a joke.

"This will scream 'California girl,'" he'd said through his laughter when she'd opened the gift and her jaw had hit the floor.

The truth was, Cathy couldn't feel any less like a California girl in it. Despite being vegan for eight years, despite hours of daily yoga, her body just wanted to stay curvy. Underneath the fat were muscles, but in the wetsuit Cathy felt like a giant hot-pink ball of human flesh.

She missed him physically, as though she were a bird and her wings no longer worked without him. Maybe being in the ocean would help her connect with him. Find his spirit, ask it to go back to him. Maybe he was just lost somewhere out there, in the waves, and if she found him, she could help him return to his body.

Or maybe that was just a bunch of New Age crap.

Cathy gathered her hair into a messy bun, took her surfboard and walked down a rocky path towards the white beach hidden between the hills.

She spotted them from above. Cathy was willing to sell her soul to the Devil for a chance that they wouldn't notice her. But even the Devil couldn't hide her glowing hot-pink wetsuit. The five of them stopped before Cathy, four middle-aged men and Miranda. The guys were not in the best form, a couple of them with beer bellies. Jason was the most chiseled. Miranda was petite but had the physique of a bodybuilder and the tan of someone who spent hours in the sun. They scowled at her.

"What are you doing here?" Miranda said. "You're not allowed on the beach."

Cathy curled into a ball internally. Most surfers weren't like these guys. Most were like Brad, laid-back, traveling the world and enjoying the ocean. Miranda and the gang never left California. They'd grown up with one of the most magnificent beaches in the world right in their backyard, and they refused to share it. Unfortunately, surf localists weren't just a problem here. And the police couldn't do anything about them, nor could public protests.

But she wouldn't let them get to her this time. "Are you continuing your bullying, even after what happened to Brad? Seriously, you guys are like teenagers on a schoolyard. Grow up."

"Maybe so," Jason said. "But someone needs to protect our beach. Look at this." He swept a hand towards the beach. There were just three people in the water and no one except Cathy and the group on the beach. The bay was spectacular. Smooth sand, tall cliffs, and waves breaking against a point. "Why do you think Sonada isn't crowded like Malibu or El Porto? Because we protect it. Brad grew up here, too. He became a world champion being trained on these waves, in this freedom. If we allow every tourist here, you wouldn't be able to spit without hitting someone."

"Especially if you guys had opened your damn yoga and surfing school," Miranda said.

Yes, that was the reason they had driven him away from the beach, making him choose, Cathy or the group. Cathy or the beach.

He'd chosen Cathy.

Fight for yourself, Cathy. Stand up to them like he did.

"You guys aren't even sorry," she said. "Don't you see that he almost died because of you?"

Miranda shook her head. Jason looked down, his nostrils flaring.

"If you want to blame anyone for what happened to him," Miranda said. "Blame yourself. He was one of us. Our world champion. He'd never have left the beach if it wasn't for you. You planted the idea of opening that school in his head."

Cathy's throat clenched.

"Stop it, Miranda," Jason said. "There won't be a school anymore. Not without Brad."

Cathy's eyes blurred, her chest tightened. He was right. Not without Brad.

Jason looked at Cathy, and his face softened. "Just for him, stay and surf. Only today, though. Don't come back. It's hard for all of us."

He tugged Miranda after him, and the five of them walked away.

Were they seriously blaming her for Brad's accident? Worse, were they right? Her stomach twisted with doubt. If he hadn't chosen her, he'd likely still be well and whole, living his life.

On shaky legs, her arms like cooked noodles, she walked to the ocean. The crash of the waves familiar and soothing, Cathy walked into the cool water, her feet numbing from the cold. She set the board on the water, jumping over waves, then lay on it and began paddling into the open sea. The wind wasn't strong today and the waves weren't the best for surfing. But she didn't really want to surf anyway. She just wanted to be out on the water.

To connect with Brad.

With the beach far behind her, she stopped paddling and sat on the board, legs hanging from either side.

Maybe Brad's soul was somewhere around here. Maybe it was deep down at the bottom of the sea where he'd hit his head. Maybe Cathy should dive and see if she could find it.

Or maybe she should just dive and stay down. Period.

Maybe she and Brad would be together again.

She looked down into the dark blue water. Maybe she should just let go.

Someone splashed cold water in her face. Cathy gasped, her eyes burning from the salt. She looked up and through stinging lids, saw an old lady on a board.

Cathy was so astounded she almost fell off when a wave rocked her.

"Hello, dear," the lady said.

She was dressed in a black wetsuit with salad-green stripes. Her white hair was gathered in a small bun at her neck, and her eyes were the most peculiar color—well, they were changing color, it seemed. Or maybe they were all colors at the same time.

"H-hello," Cathy said.

The woman lifted her face to the sun. "Lovely day, isn't it?"

Cathy looked around, just to make sure the lady was talking to her. "Yes. It is. I'm sorry, are you okay? Do you need any help getting back to shore?"

"Oh no, dear. I'm wonderful. It is you who needs help."

Cathy looked down at the board. Maybe it was damaged and she hadn't noticed? But it looked perfectly fine.

"What are you talking about?"

"Dying here is not your destiny."

Cathy considered herself a spiritual person. She felt there was a higher power in the universe and believed in the law of attraction. She taught yoga.

But she had never experienced the feeling she was having now. It was as if cold sparks of electricity crawled under her skin. "How do you know?" she asked.

"You won't find his soul down there, dear. And even if you did, that wouldn't bring him back."

A painful knot formed in Cathy's throat, and she forced herself to inhale deeply and slowly, then counted to four, then breathed out again counting to four. She might be crazy, but there was something about this woman.

"Can you help me get him back?" Cathy said.

"Oh, but sweetheart, you can't help him. However, there is a man you *can* help. The man who is destined for you."

Cathy frowned. "Do you mean Brad?"

The woman smiled as if Cathy was a cute but silly child. "It's not Brad, although Brad is partly him." She shook her head. "Less talk, more action."

She unzipped a key pocket on her thigh and produced a strangely large object for the size of the pocket. How had she gotten it in there?

The object glistened in her hands like gold. Well, it was gold.

A spindle.

Its smooth surface was covered with beautiful engravings that Cathy recognized from the Norse mythology that had always interested her.

She looked into the serene wrinkled face of the woman. "Who are you?"

"I am exactly what you are afraid to believe I am. Now, sweetheart, we do not have much time. There is a man who needs you to save him. In return, he will save you."

The woman held out the spindle to Cathy, and, bewildered, Cathy watched it.

"Hurry," the woman pressed. "The battle is about to begin, and then it'll be too late."

All this sounded too strange even for Cathy, but she couldn't stop staring at the spindle. Her hand reached out of its own accord. When she touched the spindle, a soft meditative state enveloped her.

The world around her began disappearing—the sky, the coast, the lady. All that was left was the surf splashing and the lady's voice, "You are going to travel back in time."

And then, as if it was a wave lifting her up and throwing her down, Cathy plunged into it. The energy washed through her and carried her toward an unknown shore.

And then everything went dark.

CHAPTER TWO

"Give up, you fools!" Ubba roared. He stood on Andor's left, the chains of his rich brynja glistening in the gray light of the windy winter day. Across the pebbled beach from the Viking forces stood the formation of Anglo-Saxons. "We are almost twice as many as you." Then he added something else in the Saxon tongue, which Andor did not speak.

A man in rich armor among the enemies, Ealdorman Odda, yelled something back which made Ubba guffaw in a gloating way, and he said to his men, "He cannot swear for shit."

The men chuckled. Smirking, Ubba glanced up, above Andor's head, to where the wind from the ocean played with the raven banner. If the raven flapped its wings, the battle would be successful. If it did not, the battle would end in defeat. Fridstein held the banner, standing in the first row of the formation, to Andor's right side.

Andor took in the surroundings. The cliffs rose almost as tall as those in Norway. On top of one cliff stood the Cynwit hillfort and beyond it the path into Wessex.

Under the winter sky, between the Vikings and the Anglo-Saxons, the angry sea sent tall gray waves crashing. To their left, twenty-three ships rocked where they had come in close to shore. They had brought seven hundred men. While the north-eastern territories belonged to Norsemen, the western coast of Wessex was almost untouched by the Great Heathen Army and ripe for the taking. King Alfred, that cowardly bastard, was hiding somewhere around here after a devastating defeat. There was no better moment to take Wessex, the last standing Anglo-Saxon kingdom.

"The raven does not flap its wings," Ubba said, his jaw tense, his nostrils flared.

Andor glanced up. The white triangular banner with an embroidered black raven sagged despite the strong wind. It had a rounded outside edge on which there hung several tabs with runes. Rumor had it, three of Ubba's sisters, the daughters of legendary Ragnar Lothbrok had made the banner. The three of them were völvas, and they had whispered the magic of Odin into their work.

When Andor had asked Ubba if the rumor was true, Ubba had only shrugged and changed the subject with a mischievous look on his face.

But Ubba believed the banner's premonitions. And so far, it had never been wrong.

Andor did not think this banner could control the outcome of today's battle. Though he had no doubt it could undermine the morale of their commander and of the whole horde.

"Ubba, do not think anything of it," Andor said. "We cannot lose. Not now. We are twice as many as them. The men are ready. Let us take Wessex."

Ubba nodded and touched Mjölnir, the Thor's hammer pendant on his neck. He raised his spear, signaling the beginning of the battle.

"Odin, take these dogs as my sacrifice to you!"

The beach filled with the roar of seven hundred men. Andor joined, letting the battle fury kindle in his gut, then spread in his veins like wildfire, burning away the memory of Svana, and the pain of losing her.

If Ubba's superstitious belief was right, and the battle would finally bring death to Andor, he would welcome it.

The Anglo-Saxons assumed a defensive position, and Ubba was about to throw the spear that would start the battle when pink flashed between the two armies. Andor had never seen this color in his life. It was like the pink of the sky at sea before the sunrise—but so much more intense, it hurt his eyes.

Right between the Viking and the Anglo-Saxon forces stood a woman. She was covered with bright-pink skin, except for her face, her hands, and her feet. She was tall and muscular and blonde.

An elfin? A giantess? A Valkyrie?

If she was a Valkyrie, Ubba was right—they were doomed, and she had come to take the dead.

Andor was not the only one seeing her, because the roar of seven hundred Norsemen around him died. Their weapons sank. They stared at her.

The enemy took advantage or their astonishment and launched at them.

The battle began. The spear did not fly. Odin did not bless them.

"Shieldwall!" Ubba cried.

As Norsemen began grouping into shieldwalls, Andor sank behind his shield, the strange woman disappearing from his vision. Battle fury stewed within him.

He had said it himself—all there was left for him, was battle.

CATHY WANTED TO SCREAM, but terror paralyzed her throat. She emerged on a pebble beach between a gray sea and sky, giant cliffs lining the shore. It was so cold—so cold, that the wind turned her into an icicle.

Worse, she stood between two medieval armies. One group looked like English knights, the other—like Vikings.

Her breath froze in her throat and the ground sank under her feet, but she saw one face that made heat rush through her, melting the fear away.

Brad's face.

He stood among the Vikings, in the first row, staring at her, like the rest of the horde of bearded men behind him, with an open mouth. He held a round Viking shield and a sword. His hair was long and wavy, the lower part of his face hidden under a beard.

"But I just shaved you," she whispered to herself. What an idiot she was. As if that was the most important thing right now!

How about the fact that he wasn't in a coma anymore?

But then the knights roared and launched—right at the Vikings.

Right at her.

Finally, the fight-or-flight instinct kicked in. Her feet unlocked, and she flew out of the charging men's way, towards the cliffs, towards the bushes.

A Viking roared "Skjalborg!" The word rang strange in her ears, as though it was in a foreign language. Somehow she knew it meant "shieldwall." Then several similar commands echoed.

As metal and wood and men clashed behind her, she saw a cave behind the bushes in the cliff. She sprinted for it as fast as her legs could go. She ignored the pain of the pebbles digging into her feet, the burning of her lungs, until she made it to the opening. It was a small cave, barely two feet deep, and there was no way she'd be able to stand up in there. But she crawled in, and only when her back pressed against the far wall, and she was certain no one had chased her, did she allow herself to breathe.

Her ragged breath was so loud and so heavy, it echoed off the cave walls almost drowning out the sounds of the battle. Her hands shook, and she realized the soles of her bare feet hurt. When she inspected one of her feet, she found it was bruised and cut in several places from sharp pebbles, although not deeply.

The cave wall cut into Cathy's back and chilled her. It smelled like wet earth and old seaweed.

This place didn't smell like the baked saltiness of the Pacific.

Where was she?

Why was Brad dressed like a Viking warrior and about to fight hundreds of people who looked as though they'd stepped out of a British period drama?

The screams and roars and thuds of weapons rang loudly on the beach. If anything, they were getting closer to Cathy.

That old lady on the surfboard who'd appeared out of nowhere in the middle of the sea—who was she? Then that golden spindle with Viking patterns.

Cathy's skin chilled.

She had never tried LSD, although she had friends in the yoga circles who had sworn it had therapeutic qualities. Had there been some sort of hallucinogen on the surface of the spindle? The lady had said, "You are going to travel back in time." But that was impossible, wasn't it?

That man looked so much like Brad...

Could this be an alternate reality like in one of those sci-fi shows? And in this reality, Brad was alive and healthy...and a Viking?

The lady had said something about helping a man—did Cathy need to save him?

Oh God—what if she failed and he got wounded again?

She crouched and crawled to the mouth of the cave, into the light, but couldn't see anything from behind the bushes. Carefully, she got out and peered from behind the bush.

What she saw turned her world upside down.

Being raised in a good family, in a safe environment, she had only seen death and violence on TV.

Now, men lay with open guts, cleaved skulls and wounds in their chests, throats, arms, and legs. Others fought, swords and shields clashing. Bile rose in her throat, terror staking her feet to the ground.

This was no movie, no studio tour, no game.

People really were dying right in front of her eyes.

Just when vomit rose to her mouth, she saw Brad. He chased a man in armor who was holding a crumpled and torn banner in his hand. Brad grabbed him and knocked him to the ground, then kicked the man and drove his sword into his neck.

Cathy gripped the branches of the bush so as not to fall back on her ass.

Her Brad would never do that.

Her Brad was a vegan. He hated the idea of killing other living things.

A warrior sneaked up behind Brad and dove the pommel of

his sword into Brad's head. Brad turned and swung his sword, but it looked awkward, like his arms were cooked spaghetti. He collapsed bonelessly to the ground.

The warrior bent down to finish him off. A loud shout from the battlefield stilled the man. He straightened and ran to join a couple of fighters.

On the beach, men still fought, but many Vikings were running back to the ships. Cathy's blood chilled. If they lost, the English would probably soon come and see that Brad was still alive.

Cathy had to help him.

She couldn't let him get hurt for a second time.

Her heart was racing. Staying low, she moved to Brad, hooked her hands under his armpits and pulled.

Oh man, he was huge and heavy. He barely moved.

Cathy pulled as hard as she could, and his body inched along. She had to be quick, they'd see her any minute.

But luckily, they didn't. She managed to pull him into the cave—she had to sit him up, he was so big. With him in there, she barely had any space for herself.

She had to see how badly wounded he was. She felt his pulse, and even though it was weak, it was there.

She quickly scanned his body for wounds but saw only scratches and bruises.

Finally, his head.

The back of his head was bleeding, and the wound looked almost like the one he had gotten while surfing.

Cathy's hands shook. She needed something to stop it, but she had absolutely nothing with her except for the wetsuit and her car key in the secret pocket. Maybe there was something outside. She crawled out through the bushes, and saw the banner clasped in a warrior's hand. When she was sure no one was nearby, she reached out and grasped the linen. Back in the cave, she beat the soil and grass from the cloth and pressed it against Brad's wound.

She looked at his peaceful face, just like countless days at the hospital, wishing, praying, that he'd move, twitch and wake up.

"I believe in the magic of life," she said. "I believe that you'll be all right."

Then she began repeating the words like a prayer. She began rocking, after a time, in meditation.

Cathy didn't know how much time passed. But the sounds of battle stopped outside, and more light came into the cave—the sun had moved to the west and would start setting soon enough.

She was used to waiting and looking at every eyelash, every little vein on his eyelids for a movement.

Which had never happened in the whole year he'd been in the hospital.

Now, his eyelids flew open, and his blue eyes stared right at her.

CHAPTER THREE

SHE WAS LOVELY. Big gray eyes with long, thick eyelashes; soft, rosy cheeks; a mouth like a flower in full bloom; and pale freckles that spilled across her nose like gold dust. Her blonde hair was tied high in a knot on top of her head—a warrior's hairstyle—exposing her face fully to him.

Her expression was raw and open. Vulnerable. She looked at him with concern and something resembling wonder. Elation.

And although it was dark here, the bright-pink skin that started right under her chin glowed like the last sunrise before Ragnarok, hurting his eyes.

"Valkyrie?" he croaked.

She frowned. "What?"

He blinked, his eyes adjusting to the light of the cave. "Valkyrie, did you come to take me to Valhalla?"

Her lips curved in a sweet, sad smile. She cupped his jaw, the touch feather-light. "Poor baby, you hit your head hard. Again. At least you're not in a coma." She looked around. "Maybe this really is some weird alternate reality, and I'm speaking some weird language I don't remember learning." She looked at him and her eyes softened. "But you're alive. And I'm here, with you. And that's all that matters."

Andor blinked. Her words made little sense and made his head hurt. He attempted to sit upright, but his head spun and ached, and bile rose in his throat. He became aware of the cold, rough surface he was sitting on, and sharp rocks digging into his flesh.

This could not be the way to Valhalla. He was not dying.

And this woman was not a Valkyrie.

"Brad, honey, don't move." She leaned closer to him. "You've lost blood, and you might have a concussion."

Whoever this stranger was, at least she was not trying to kill him.

"What is Brad?" he said.

Her face fell. "It's your name. Isn't it?"

"No."

Something was wrong with her. Andor pushed off the wall of the cave to sit up. A big mistake. The ground shifted like the deck of a ship in a storm. He leaned back and touched the spot on the back of his head from which the pain was radiating. His fingers found linen instead of hair. She must have bandaged his wound.

"What is your name, then?" she said, her voice shaking.

"Andor Thornsson."

She licked her lips, her chest rising and falling faster. "Do you remember me?"

He squinted at her. "I remember. You came out of thin air on the beach. I thought you were a Valkyrie. All my men did."

Her frown deepened.

"If you are not a Valkyrie, to all gods, who are you?"

"My name is Cathy," she said. "I'm your fiancée."

Loki's stinky feet, his betrothed?

If he could stand up and leave this madwoman, he would. But his head ached as though a drunken giant was stomping on it.

"I do not have a betrothed," he said through gritted teeth. "Stop this nonsense."

She pressed her lips together, then forced out a smile. "I see. If this is a parallel reality where you have a different name and wear some sort of medieval armor and"—she glanced helplessly at the mouth of the cave—"fight like a barbarian, I understand that you wouldn't remember me."

Then she turned to him, her eyes shining, almost sparkling. And with conviction, she said, "But I remember you."

Andor let out a low growl. The female annoyed him with her strange words and confused him with her strange pink body... He looked down. It was not her skin. It was something resembling clothes. Why did she not wear a woman's dress?

If anything, this resembled armor, although armor of cloth made little sense. Or maybe some sort of armor that looked like it was made of cloth. Maybe dwarfs had made this armor as unbreakable as Gleipnir, the chains that held the giant wolf Fenrir.

She was the reason the battle that was supposed to be an easy victory had turned into a complete defeat.

Ubba—

The memory flashed in his mind—Ubba falling dead, killed by the leader of the Anglo-Saxons.

Anger roared in Andor's gut, mixed with the deepest sadness he had felt since Hvaldalen was burned. Since Svana...

It was this woman's fault.

He sat upright. This time his head did not spin as much. Maybe his anger towards her gave him strength.

"You...it was all because of you. You appeared, and the

Anglo-Saxons used our astonishment to attack... Where did you come from?"

Cathy blinked. "From Los Angeles, California."

Insolent woman. Throwing those strange words at him again. "Because of you, we lost—"

Had they lost? Andor had to see.

"But Brad—" she began. He ignored her.

With great difficulty, and through raging pain, Andor moved on all fours and crawled towards the exit of the cave.

"Brad—I mean, Andor, wait—"

When he went outside, the sunlight hurt his eyes. He waited a moment, and when his vision returned, he crawled to look around the thicket blocking his view of the beach. The sight made his stomach drop.

Countless bodies covered the beach—the bodies of his warriors. Anglo-Saxon soldiers walked around piercing those who might still be alive and looking for their wounded. Ubba's ships, including five of Andor's own, were gone.

He tightened his fists, then turned to her. "You brought our defeat."

She gasped. "I didn't do anything! It's not like I chose to teleport to the middle of a battle."

Then her eyes widened as she looked behind him. Andor looked in that direction. An Anglo-Saxon was coming at them, his bloody sword glistening.

Andor reached to his belt for his sword but found empty air.

"Where is my sword?" he barked, looking around.

"There!" Cathy pointed to his left. A few steps away lay a dead Anglo-Saxon, and next to him, Dragon's Trouble.

With a head that felt like it was about to split, Andor rose to his feet and staggered a few steps. Pebbles rustled under his enemy's boots, and the soldier roared right next to him. Andor picked up the sword and whirled, just in time to deflect the Anglo-Saxon's weapon.

Rising, Andor swung his sword, aiming for the man's side. But he was weak and slow, and the Saxon managed to deflect him.

The man came again and again, and all Andor could do was duck and evade and divert. White-hot pain seared Andor as the warrior stabbed him in the thigh. Cathy shrieked, and the Saxon looked in her direction, exposing his neck. Andor brought his sword around in one sweeping move that sent pain shooting through his whole body and cut off the man's head.

Then he fell to his knees, panting. The world around him spun, and the ground beneath his knees shifted, then sank. Something cool and hard pressed against his ear as the ground stood vertically and the sky and sea as well.

"Andor! Andor!" the muffled female voice reached him.

His ears rung, and his body drooped and crumpled, heavy and powerless.

And then he sank into the dark sea of oblivion.

CHAPTER FOUR

Brad collapsed.

Not Brad. Andor.

Her man fell, blood flowing out of the new wound in his hip. Cathy didn't even have time to react to the sight of the chopped off human head that rolled and bounced like a soccer ball.

"Andor!" Cathy called. "Andor!"

His eyes rolled back in his head and he was out again.

He'd lost too much blood. How had he found any strength to fight that man in the first place?

Cathy rushed to him and turned him over. She looked at his leg closely. She needed to stop the bleeding immediately, but first she needed to take him back to safety and hide him before any more warriors came for them.

She dragged Andor behind the bushes which, she hoped, provided enough cover for now. Tearing the edge off of Andor's tunic under his armor, she pressed it hard against the wound. It was on the outer side of the thigh, thank goodness, not near the groin where the artery was. The wound was deep, though, because the whole cloth was soon saturated with blood.

"Darn it, Andor!" Cathy said as she tore more of his tunic. It was covered with dirt and dust and a little hard from sea salt, really bad for an open wound. He'd obviously been on the road for a long time. But it was better than nothing.

She pressed the cloth onto the wound for a couple of minutes, but she heard voices close by, right behind the bushes. The cloth finally stopped filling with blood, and Cathy pulled Andor back into the cave.

There she felt his pulse, which was weak but steady. She'd probably need to suture his thigh wound—maybe even the one on the back of his head, too. She had never done it before, but she had gone through an advanced first aid and medical help course for surfers with Brad.

The voices came so close that she could make out what they said.

"Father Paul, this one is dead."

"Requiescat in pace," someone else said.

"I think this one is still alive," the first, younger voice said.

"Let me see." Steps, then silence. "No, he can't be, not after this neck wound. God be with you, my son. You fought bravely in the name of Christ and our king."

Cathy swallowed. They sounded like priests, or maybe monks. She had to act fast. If she was in a reality where there were medieval knights and Viking raiders, there had to be monasteries. And monks were probably the best doctors available.

She peered out of the cave, and in the space where the bushes ended, she saw the back of a wooden cart that was being pulled into the distance by a donkey, two men in brown robes walking by its side. On the cart, a man lay on a bed of straw.

The monks appeared to be gathering the wounded. She had to get Brad—Andor—to them.

Two problems. One, they'd likely recognize a Viking and call soldiers to kill him. Two, they would probably burn her as a witch or something in her pink wetsuit. Which meant, she had to get rid of anything that would betray Andor as a Viking. And take off her wetsuit and find some clothes.

She looked Andor over. She had little idea what the difference was between medieval English clothes and Viking clothes, but she had to make her best guess. The English seemed to wear metal armor, helmets, and such. Their weapons were different, too. But she imagined their clothes underneath were basically the same. So if she took Andor's armor and hid his sword, that should be enough, right? She could say she removed his armor to treat his wounds.

She carefully undid the laces of his leather breast plate and pulled it over his head. Not an easy task with a giant warrior the size of a Mr. Universe contestant—especially when she needed to avoid brushing his wounded head.

When his armor was off, the next task was to do something about her clothes. She glanced around, but the only thing she could think of was the last thing she wanted to do.

Take off a dead Saxon's clothes and put them on.

Cathy winced at the thought, but she had no time for squeamishness if she wanted to save *Andor's* life.

She moved to the bush. The monks were further away, bending over a man on the ground. Cathy ran towards the first man Andor had injured, the one who'd had the raven banner she had used to bandage Andor's head. For what felt like the hundredth time, she dragged a grown man behind the bush.

She grimaced at the sight of his pale face and the opening on his neck. How could she touch the corpse? Undress it? Wear its clothes?

Cathy didn't feel it coming, but the contents of her stomach rose, and all she could do was turn and vomit. She shook, as though she had a fever. All her instincts told her to pull away, to run.

She would gladly do that.

But she loved Brad too much, even if this version didn't know her.

She had to be strong for him. Not the weak coward she had been a year ago, when she should have insisted that Brad stay with his friends, that she could open the school without him, rather than wallowing in her insecurity and relying on Brad for courage.

Look where that had led her.

She couldn't make the same mistake again.

She briefly closed her eyes, took a cleansing breath and found her center. That helped her to let go of her fear and disgust and gain at least some strength.

She wiped her mouth, which still tasted sour. "Forgive me, whoever you are," she whispered to the dead man in front of her. Forbidding herself to think of what she was really doing, Cathy began undressing the man. Removing chain mail from a grown man was hard work, but, slowly, she managed. It must have weighed at least twenty pounds, and she was soaked in sweat and breathing heavily when she was done. Taking off the rest of his clothes was a piece of cake compared to that.

With regret, she removed her wetsuit—thankfully she wore diving shorts and a vest underneath.

Then came the hard part: putting the dead man's clothes on. The tunic smelled like unwashed body, old male sweat, and blood. The neck and the breast of the tunic were soaked in blood, and she swore the material cracked when she put it on.

Vomit rose again, and Cathy firmly decided to breathe through her mouth.

That helped. Then came the pants, which she refused to smell at all. They were made of a coarse material like hemp, but they fit her fine. In fact, all the clothes fit as though they were made for her. A depressing fact she decided not to dwell upon at the moment.

She even took off the man's wool socks and then his shoes, which were made of surprisingly soft leather and were the most comfortable thing she was wearing right now.

If she wore a man's clothes and was about to ask the monks to take her and Andor in, she couldn't do so as a woman. Thankfully, her bun was still up. If she put on the weird linen cap the dead man had on, could she pass for an overgrown teenage boy? Her breasts and hips were not that visible under this large tunic.

Maybe for the first time in her life, her height and weight would actually come in handy.

The last thing was to hide Andor's sword. She took it and went into the cave. There was a long crack in the back, and she placed the sword there, then put rocks and scattered shingles where the metal was visible.

Satisfied, she grabbed Andor and dragged him out of the cave, placing him next to the bush. She threw one last, critical glance over him and noticed an amulet around his neck, with a pendant that looked like a hammer.

This was probably for Thor or Odin or one of the other Norse gods. If it wasn't a cross, she should probably take it off of him, which she did and put it around her neck, under the tunic. Whatever it was, it made her feel closer to him in some way.

She glanced in the direction of the monks who were now quite far away, almost on the other side of the beach. But she noticed three more carts like the first and ran to the nearest one.

When she was close enough, making her voice low, she said, "Fathers."

She then realized she spoke yet another foreign language. It was different from Andor's but similar to English in some way. Was it Old English or something?

How could she speak not just one but two ancient foreign languages she had never learned? What kind of craziness was going on? And what if she suddenly lost the ability or the monks realized she was not a boy, not even a person from this time? Didn't they burn witches back then? The urge to run and hide sent her heart racing.

The two monks turned around. Too late to run.

Their heads were shaved on top, the rest of their hair in a bowl cut. Big, wooden crosses hung on their necks. One was older—he was examining a man lying on the ground—the other one was younger and looked stronger. They both eyed Cathy up and down, suspicion in their eyes.

"Yes?" said the older one.

Cathy's skin chilled, her fingers trembled. Did they recognize she was a woman? Did they recognize she didn't actually speak their language? Had she done something that betrayed that she was from a different reality—or time?

Too late now, she told herself again. She needed to help Andor, one way or another. "Help," she said, still in a low voice that she hoped would resemble a man's. "My friend's injured."

They exchanged a glance, and the older man nodded. "Where is he, son?"

Son? Cathy's shoulders relaxed, and she pointed at the bush.

"Let us go, Brother Aethelred," the older one said. They turned the donkey and followed Cathy.

CHAPTER FIVE

Through a splitting headache, Andor rose to consciousness. Above him was a darkening sky, half of it indigo, the other half golden and pink. In that golden-pink half, was a beautiful female face.

Svana.

No.

Not Svana.

Svana's eyes were green and her hair brown. The hair and eyes above him were not. And though the face was as soft and lovely, it was not hers. His heart ached at the memory that he would never see his wife's face again, and he quickly shut away the feeling and the ghosts that still haunted him.

Everything shook and swayed under him. He lay on something soft yet prickly. Wheels rumbled against the road.

The woman's gentle gaze comforted him.

"Go back to sleep," she whispered. "I've got you."

Her cool hand rested on his forehead. With an odd feeling of safety, he fell back into darkness.

When he next woke, he lay on something soft and comfortable, covered with a blanket. Through his eyelids which were still closed, light protruded and made his vision pink. It was quiet, although he thought he heard someone breathing. His hand slowly crawled under his pillow where he usually kept his scramasax.

But the short sword was not there. Slowly, he opened his eyes.

He was in a small room with a stone floor and walls. Daylight fell through a small window. A wooden cross hung on otherwise bare walls. Across the room from him, by the wall, stood a wooden bench on which slept a tall teenage boy covered with a blanket. Andor lay in a bed fit for a grown child, his feet hanging over the end.

A distant pain pounded in the back of his heavy head. His thigh throbbed and burned. He was so weak, as though he had not eaten or drunk for ages.

Every part of his body thirsted. He turned his head and saw a clay jug and a cup standing on the stone windowsill. There must be water.

Andor tried to sit up, but his head spun and he had to hold on to the edges of the mattress, or risk falling off the bed.

"Hel," he groaned.

The boy stirred and lifted his head, revealing big gray eyes with long eyelashes.

Andor remembered those eyes. It was not a boy. It was that madwoman, Cathy, who claimed to be betrothed to him.

Then he remembered fighting. He had thought he'd died, but here he was with this strange woman again.

"Water," he croaked.

"Right away." She rushed to the window and poured water into a cup, then held it for him. Andor gulped the cool liquid down and did not think he had ever tasted anything as good.

While she was refilling the cup, he glanced at her again.

The bright-pink armor was gone, and she wore the clothes of a Saxon man. She smelled like one, too—an unwashed one.

She gave him another cup, and he drank it.

"More?" she asked, but he shook his head.

She sat on the edge of his bed with a sheepish look.

"Where am I?" he asked.

"Wilham Monastery."

Andor tried to raise himself on his elbows but his arms were too weak. The name sounded familiar.

"Someone needed to patch you up," she said. "And there doesn't seem to be proper hospitals. Or electricity." She stood up and walked to the window, peering out of it. "Or cars. Or running water. They brought you here on a cart pulled by a donkey."

"Why did you bring me into the midst of the enemy?" he spat. "You should have left me to die."

Cathy cringed. "Oh no, my friend. Not on my watch. I've almost lost one version of you back home. I'm not losing this one."

"Is this more talk about me being your betrothed? Because I am not him."

She crossed her arms over her chest and lifted her chin. "Maybe not, Andor. Or Brad. Or whoever you are. But I'm not letting you die."

"Where are my weapons? My armor?"

She shrugged. "I had to hide your sword. I was afraid they'd recognize you as a Viking. You are a Viking, right?"

"Of course I am a Viking." He glowered. "You insolent woman. If I had any strength left, I'd bend you over my knee and—"

Her jaw fell open, her face reddening. His gaze crawled down her body. Even under the man's clothing he could see long, straight legs, the generous curves of her breasts and hips. Her lips must be soft and her arse must be a feast.

He turned away, angry and helpless.

"Bend me over your knee?" she said. "Excuse me, how about showing me a little appreciation for saving your life? I'm wearing a dead man's clothes for you—and you want to punish me?"

He turned back to her. "I never asked you to save my life. And taking me weaponless into the midst of the enemy is just like killing me, only slower. So, no, I am not grateful. Tyr would be more grateful to Fenrir for biting off his hand."

She pressed her lips tightly together. "For the record, you are not alone. You have me."

"I do not have you. I do not want you. I am alone."

She seemed to be hurt by his words, her eyes dampening, but she raised her chin.

"Oh yeah?" she said. "You are alone, huh? Do you speak Old English?"

"Old English?"

"Anglo-Saxon or whatever."

He sighed. "No."

"Then you need me, mister. I told the monks you were a mute English soldier so that they would treat you. So if they come in, not a word from you, do you hear me?"

Andor grimaced. The plan was both simple and bold. The woman had Loki's mind. Maybe he'd sent her.

"Who are you, anyway?" Andor said.

She sighed and walked around the room, kicking the dust on the floor. "No one. I—I'm not sure what happened, to be honest. Okay, I'll tell you what I think happened, and if you believe I'm crazy, well, join the club. Or maybe you can tell me what you think. And give me a tip about how to go back. Because I must go back."

She sat on the bench across from his bed, leaning forward and pressing her elbows into her knees. She picked at her fingernails and chewed on her lower lip, making it a very agreeable dark-pink color.

Andor would have felt much better about the whole situation if he was fully dressed, but he appeared to be at her mercy, and he might as well find out exactly how crazy she was.

"Talk," he said.

"Okay. Here goes. Based on everything I have seen since yesterday, I think I probably came from the future."

Andor blinked. Out of all explanations that he could possibly imagine, he had never thought he would hear this one.

Seeing his face, Cathy hurried on. "Or maybe from an alternate reality."

No. This was the most insane explanation.

Indeed, he was in the hands of a madwoman. A pretty one. But a mad one.

And the sooner he left her company the better.

But being powerless and injured, there was little he could do to protect himself—against her or even English monks. Truthfully, he needed her right now, just until he could stand on his feet again. He needed to pretend he believed her until she got him out of here alive. Then he would make her take him to wherever she'd hidden Dragon's Trouble. After that, he'd leave her and head back to York, to Ubba—

No. Andor's mind went blank.

Ubba was dead.

His commander had fallen. Andor closed his eyes briefly, his lungs tightening, something cold and nasty slithering in his gut.

What now?

If he had a home—

But he did not. No reason to dwell on things he had no intention of changing.

He would go to York and find his men and would fight for the second strongest leader in the Anglo-Saxon lands, Guthrum.

Anything to forget the sucking, heavy darkness that enveloped him every time even a small echo of a thought about Svana and home crept through his mind.

He looked at Cathy, who was staring at him with raised brows.

"Say something. What do you think?" she said.

He cleared his throat. "I think I believe you."

She narrowed her eyes. "Really? Even I don't really believe me. I keep trying to think of another explanation, but so far these two are the best ones I've got."

"What happened before you"— he coughed—"traveled in time...or to this world."

"Well, I got some bad news yesterday morning," she said, her voice breaking. "And I went to the beach because I wanted to connect to Brad. I went surfing, well not really, just took my surfboard and paddled into the ocean."

Andor nodded as though he understood what she meant. He had no idea what a surfboard was. He imagined some sort of a boat.

"There was this strange old lady." Cathy stood up and began walking around the room again, seeming agitated. "It was so bizarre, you know? It was as if she appeared out of nowhere. We began talking, and she said something about not being able to help Brad. But that I'd need to help a Viking. And then she gave me a golden spindle."

Andor cocked his head. Golden spindle? Norns had golden spindles. But what wouldn't Loki whisper to a mad person?

"I was so stupid to touch it. I shouldn't have, but I did.

Then something happened to my body, as if I was being washed into somewhere, as though a wave grasped me and took me with it. But not just physically. Metaphysically. You know?"

He did not. But he nodded.

She nodded, too. "Okay. And then next thing I knew, I was standing on that beach, between you guys and those guys. And then...well, you know the rest."

She stopped walking and looked at him, picking her nails. "I thought at first I was on drugs. Then I figured maybe it was some sort of an alternate reality. But your wounds are real. So are the swords and the walls. And this seems like the same world I came from, but far in the past. There really is no electricity, no cars—no nothing! What else can this be but time travel? What do you think?"

Andor growled. She kept asking him what he thought, expecting him to help her. He did not want to help her. He did not want anything to do with her except for using her to get out of here alive.

"What do I think?" he asked, rage boiling in his weak body. "I think that Loki stole your mind. I think that I want you to leave me alone. And I think that I condemn every minute spent with the woman who was the reason my people lost, my commander is dead, and I lie helpless among enemies. I think I want nothing to do with you."

The woman's eyes widened and filled with tears. Her chin shook like a child's; her lips pouted and trembled. She broke into tears, turned around, and stormed out of the chamber, finally granting him his wish.

Only the relief Andor had hoped to feel did not come.

Instead, he found that he wanted to go after her and offer her comfort.

"Loki's hairy balls," he muttered.

CHAPTER SIX

Andor was not Brad.

If Cathy'd had any doubts in the beginning, after his hurtful words, she knew it. Brad wasn't capable of hurting her like that. Not her, not anyone.

Andor was.

Cathy went for a long walk after their chat because she could not stay in the same room with him anymore. He made her feel awkward, different. But not different in a good way. Different in a disgusting loser way.

Just like the surf localists had made her feel, just like her Hollywood agent dad, her beauty queen mom and her social-media influencer sister.

Like a drunk elephant in a china shop.

But Andor was worse. Because she had actually risked her life to save his.

Because he looked just like Brad, she had assumed she could trust him.

But she was wrong. Clearly.

And yet, she needed him. If the old lady really had sent

Cathy back in time to save him, Cathy had accomplished the mission and needed to find a way back to LA. If she didn't get back in time, Brad's parents might get permission to disconnect his life support. Her shoulders tightened, fear rooting her to the spot.

She needed to find out if Andor had any idea how she could get back. She wouldn't risk anything for him anymore, though.

When Cathy returned to Andor's chamber after her walk, the young monk, Brother Aethelred, was there, changing the dressing on Andor's wound.

Cathy stopped at the doors, watching Andor's furious face and bulging eyes with horror. He looked as though he was about to tear the poor monk apart.

"Brother Aethelred," she said. "Is everything all right?"

The monk turned around. "Ah. Cathan." He returned to his work. "Your friend's wound looks well so far. I am impressed he has not screamed while I was redressing the wound."

Cathy cleared her throat and made an effort to deepen her voice. "It is not the first time he got injured."

"Ah, well, I can imagine, with him being a Northman," he said.

Cathy froze, her teeth clenching till her jaw ached.

"What?" she said, her voice a rasp.

Andor frowned and looked at her with worry.

"Do not alarm our friend while I tell you what I am about to tell you," the monk said in the same calm voice, his hands applying a poultice to Andor's wound. "I recognize him. He was the first Northman I ever saw. Three years ago, he raided our monastery and took the jeweled Bible which was sent to us from Rome. He did not kill anyone, but he did injure the brothers who were protecting the Bible. He made quite a fearful impression on me. I shall never forget this face."

Cold sweat crawled down Cathy's spine. What did this

mean? Would Aethelred give them to the local authorities? She tightened her fists, her arms and legs as hard as wood.

"Cathan, please ask him where the Bible is, the one that he took."

Cathy swallowed a hard knot and translated, choosing her words carefully, afraid that one slip would set Andor or Aethelred off. Andor's eyes widened with alarm as he listened to her, but he kept silent.

When he didn't answer, the monk pressed, "Tell him I just want to know. It was the greatest spiritual treasure that I had ever seen, and I just want to make sure the book is whole."

Cathy translated, and Andor responded, "The book was fine the last time I saw it. Ubba sold it to the king of Mercia for land."

When Cathy told Aethelred what Andor had said, his face relaxed into a serene smile. He nodded, picked up the bowl of water and the bloody cloth he had used and stood up. He turned to walk away, but Cathy called after him. "Are you going to have us killed?"

He turned. "No. He is a patient. A wounded man, a human. God wants us to forgive sins—ours and the sins of others. That is what I will do."

Relief flooded her chest, air filling her lungs. "Thank you."

"Ask him why he is not furious with me for taking the Bible," Andor said. "Why does he heal me? Why did he not tell the local warlord about me?"

Cathy did as he asked and translated the monk's response. "He says he has forgiven you. He was angry with you and also afraid of you. He considered not helping you when he recognized you, but that would have been the easy thing to do. The more difficult thing was to forgive you. You are a human being, Viking or not, and so is he. He wishes you only the best and asks you not to kill any more of his countrymen."

Andor's face paled, his eyes widening.

With his chin, Aethelred pointed at the bench where two bowls with stew stood, along with half a loaf of dark bread, and a small bowl with butter. "He must eat. He lost much blood. I am not surprised he can barely lift a finger."

"I'll make sure he eats," she said. "Thank you, Brother Aethelred."

The monk gave a small nod and walked out. Cathy crossed her arms over her chest. Despite her anger at Andor, she noticed his paleness and the dark circles under his eyes, and worry for him knotted her stomach.

"What?" he asked.

"Aethelred told me you must eat to regain your strength."

"Then let me eat."

Of course she'd give him his food in a minute, but a small, vengeful part of her wanted him to know how much he'd hurt her.

"I thought you didn't want my help. I thought you didn't want anything to do with me."

"Fine." He shifted to sit up, then hung his legs over the edge of the bed and threw the blanket off. He stopped for a moment, grasping the mattress and breathing hard. Cathy suppressed the impulse to scold him and make him go back to bed. He shook his head as though to shake off a dream. After a few breaths, Andor rose to his feet. He wore only a tunic that reached the middle of his thighs. Cathy couldn't help but admire his muscular legs, even though his thigh was bandaged. He took a step, but his bad leg collapsed under his weight. Cathy barely managed to catch him before he reached the floor.

"Go back to bed," she said. If she'd given him his food in the first place, he wouldn't have fallen.

She helped Andor get back, then brought him the bowl

with stew, which smelled delicious, and the butter. She split the loaf of bread in two and gave him one. Her stomach grumbled. She'd eaten some bread last night when they'd arrived, but, being vegan, refused the cottage cheese and milk. It looked like today she was going to eat only bread again.

Andor attacked the food, shoving the pieces of meat, parsnips, cabbage, and leeks into his mouth. He glanced at her. "Are you not hungry?"

Cathy bit into her dark bread, which was not fresh. "I'm eating."

"Just bread?"

"I'm vegan."

Andor frowned. "Who?"

"I don't eat any animal products."

He raised his eyebrows. "Do you get sick?"

"No."

"Then why?"

"It's healthier, for one. Second, because I don't want to take part in murdering and torturing animals. Plus, reducing meat consumption helps battle climate change."

Andor shook his head. "Loki did steal your mind. Who told you that not eating meat brings health? How will you support your strength without meat, without the fat that milk and cheese and butter have?"

"In the future, there are plenty of plant products that give you the same nutrients."

Andor returned to his food. "Maybe you are telling the truth," he mumbled through a full mouth. "No warrior would ever consider avoiding meat and butter. Are you going to eat that?" He nodded with his chin towards the second bowl of stew.

Cathy gave it to him, though her mouth watered. Ah, what

she wouldn't give for a vegan ramen noodle soup. "I'm not a warrior."

"No? You look like a shield-maiden. Who are you, then?"

Cathy was not sure if this was a compliment or an insult. Andor's gorgeous eyes traveled up and down her body, igniting her skin under her clothes. Did he approve of her being a female warrior? Surely not. Hadn't feminine women always been considered more attractive?

"I teach yoga."

"What?"

"Yoga helps strengthen physical, mental and spiritual abilities. It's from India."

Andor stopped chewing and studied her. "You speak my language and yet your words make no sense. Why do people do *yoga*?"

"To stay fit, to connect with their inner self. To live a happier life."

Andor shook his head. "To stay fit, you train as a warrior or work hard on the farm. You make a sacrifice to keep close to the gods. And you play a hnefatafl if you want to stay mentally sharp. What you are describing sounds like a waste of time."

Again, he was insulting her, rousing in her the compulsive need to make him like her, approve of her, tell her that she was doing great. The way Brad had always praised her. "It's not a waste of time. There's always a waiting list for my classes. People love me. I help them decompress from their office jobs and stay fit and healthy."

He snorted and returned to his bowl. "Maybe you are from the future. Even Loki wouldn't be able to come up with this nonsense."

Cathy clenched her hand around the bread she was holding. She suppressed the urge to throw it at him. Keep calm for

Brad, she reminded herself. She needed to find out how to get back.

"Look," she said. "Let's pretend for a moment that I'm telling the truth. I traveled in time from the future, and now I need to find a way to get back. And I must go back as soon as possible or my fiancé, Brad, might die. What do I do?"

He frowned. "Was he wounded in a battle?"

"He was wounded while surfing. He—he's in a coma. I mean, paralyzed, and they keep him alive, although unconscious. But his parents want to stop his life support, and I'm the only one who doesn't."

Andor let out a long sigh and shook his head. "You are lucky you are pretty. How does that fiancé of yours endure your mad speeches?"

A flush of heat broke through her face, and, unable to stop herself, she threw the bread at him. He laughed when it hit him in the shoulder. How could he give a compliment and yet insult her at the same time?

"More for me." He took the piece.

Cathy stomped her foot. "I'm not crazy. And Brad loves me."

"Like I said. Pretty."

Cathy grunted. She needed to keep cool. She took a long, slow breath, filling her lower lungs then upper lungs. She held her breath and counted to three then slowly exhaled. Better. Now she could think again.

"What do you suggest I do?" she asked.

He studied her and warmth spread through her skin where his eyes touched her. "All right. If you were telling the truth, it sounds like a Norn sent you here by giving you her golden spindle."

Cathy frowned. "A Norn? Does she have something to do

with destiny? I think I remember that name from Norse mythology."

"Yes. Norns spin people's fates."

Cathy covered her cheeks with her hands. "Destiny... Surely, my destiny is not back in the Viking Age! I belong with Brad. I must go back. How do I do that?"

Andor shrugged one shoulder. "I am not a gothi or a völur. I do not know."

"What is a gothi, and what is a völur?"

"Are we still playing the game where you claim you do not know basic things? All right, let us keep pretending. A gothi is a priest, a völur is a witcher."

"Where do I find those?"

"There is a völva—a witch, a seeress—in Jorvik."

"Jorvik." Cathy frowned, her mind recognized the word and translated it. "York?"

"The Anglo-Saxons call it Eoforwic. We conquered the city when we started the invasion twelve years ago. Now it is our capital here, one of the three largest cities in Bretland."

Cathy nodded. "All right. Then that's where I'll go. Is it far?"

"That is where *I* shall go. On foot, I imagine it might take two weeks. My men and I sailed from there."

She wrapped her arms around herself. "Then we should go together."

"If you must indulge your fantasies then do so, woman. Without me."

Cathy swallowed. "You need me. You can't make it through enemy territory without speaking the language. Pretending you're a mute will only get you so far. I'll be your interpreter. I'll help conceal that you're a Viking. And you seem to know the way."

"I do not know the way, only the direction. And I told you I shall not connect my destiny with you. I will go alone."

Cathy would have backed down under normal circumstances. But right now, she needed to use every method possible to get to Brad.

"Alone, huh?" she said. "Without your sword?"

His face fell. "You said you hid it. Where?"

"I'll take you there if you promise to take me with you."

"No."

"If you don't want my help, I won't lift a finger anymore."

He scowled and shook his head. "That sword was a present from my wife."

Cathy straightened. "Are you married?"

"My dead wife."

"Oh. I'm sorry."

He put the bowl aside and turned to her, his eyes burning like two blue fires. "If I allow you to come with me, I am not going to protect you. You are not going to be my responsibility. If you die or get injured or kidnapped, that will be on you. I will not save you."

The blood drained from Cathy's face. This man could not be more like her fiancé, the love of her life, on the outside, and yet he was the complete opposite on the inside. Where Brad was an angel, this man was a devil.

But Cathy had no choice. She would do anything to get back to Brad—even go on a medieval road trip with an angry Viking.

"Deal," she said.

CHAPTER SEVEN

January 12, 878 AD

"Will you stop shaking every time I stumble?" Andor grumbled.

The beautiful, crazy blonde walked beside him on the pebbled beach. He felt Cathy's sideways glances on him as though she physically touched his skin.

"I don't!" she said and took a step away from him. "Fall if you like, I don't care."

He winced a little as he avoided a large stone. "You are like a hen. I do not remember that even my mother fussed like you do."

"Well, excuse me for being a good person," she said.

His leg pained him still, and he walked slowly. After they had left the monastery earlier that morning, it had become clear he wouldn't be able to go far without some sort of help. Cathy had found a stick in a small grove, which allowed him to ease the weight off of his leg and walk.

His headaches had stopped, although the back of his head still throbbed where his scalp was sutured. And though he was still weak from blood loss, he was strong enough to start the long journey ahead.

The need to flee the monastery had become even stronger after Andor learned that this was the place he had gotten the jeweled Bible for Ubba.

The task that had kept him from getting home on time. The reason Svana had died.

Healthy or not, sitting in one place—especially that place —left him face-to-face with his memories of Hvaldalen and Svana. They tore his heart apart, blistered him, lacerated him. To escape them, he was ready to go to Helheim. No physical wound could cripple like the one in his heart.

Forgiveness.

The monk was right, it was the most difficult thing. Because it required facing the ghosts of those wronged. And he was not ready to face them yet.

The beach was clear of the dead. Pebbles crunched as Cathy and Andor made their way towards the cave. The wind blew strong. The scent of the sea and the sound of the crashing waves calmed Andor down.

"Hurry." Andor glanced at the hillfort on top of the cliff, but it was hard to see if anyone was watching them. "I do not like to be out here longer than we must."

Cathy rolled her eyes. "Buddy, I'm not the one slowing us down. We're almost there, anyway."

A few more steps and they reached the cave.

"They removed the corpse," Cathy said when they looked behind the bush in front of it.

"The corpse?"

"Yes, the one who had your banner."

Andor's blood stood still. The banner had completely escaped his mind. "Was there a raven on it?"

"Yes, I think so. Some sort of black bird."

Andor scorned himself. How could he have forgotten about it? Not only had the Viking troops lost an important battle, and Ubba, they had also lost the legendary raven banner—Odin's blessing. The sign that the gods were with them.

Andor could only imagine how dispirited they must be.

"Where is it now?" he said.

She patted the bag hanging from her shoulder. "Right here."

Andor's whole body loosened. He was ready to kiss her.

"Wow," Cathy said. "I think that is the closest thing to a smile I've ever seen on you. It suits you. You should try it more often."

"How do you have it?" he croaked.

"It was the only thing I could find to bandage your head, and then when I was getting rid of everything Viking you had on you, it had to go, too." Cathy removed the banner from the bag, then stretched it out to show him, firing up Andor's blood. "But I didn't want to leave it behind, so I took it with me."

The raven on the banner flew in dark-red caked blood. Odin must be joyous now—this was probably much more to his liking.

"You are not that crazy after all, I suppose," Andor said. "Put it back before anyone sees it. I must hurry to Jorvik to deliver it to my people."

"Why thank you, Andor," she said while wrapping the banner and putting it back in the purse. "Another compliment wrapped in an insult. You should write a book of those."

He shook his head. He knew what books were, and how the Saxons valued them. Like that Bible. He couldn't imagine wasting his time creating such a thing.

"Let us hurry, Cathy," he said. "Go get me my sword and let us be on our way."

"Yes, sir," she said and disappeared into the narrow mouth of the cave. He edged closer to it and glanced inside, marveling at her round behind as she rummaged at the back of the cave.

Time passed, and she still did not come out.

"Is something wrong?" Andor asked, his gut heavy with a bad feeling.

She kept silent for a few moments, then said. "I could swear I left it right here. Wait. Maybe here?"

Andor thumped the ground with his stick. If the sword was gone—

Dragon's Trouble's iron pommel had a snarling dragon on it, and the cross guard had interwoven patterns that looked like fire. The deer antler handle was bound with silver cords. Svana had ordered it from the best blacksmith who made the sharpest blades in the North. Andor was proud of his fine weapon, and it had never let him down in battle.

But most importantly, it was as if a part of Svana always accompanied him.

After a while, Cathy emerged from the cave.

Empty-handed.

Her cheeks were flushed, her eyes big. "I don't know what happened," she said. "It's not there, Andor. I'm sorry."

A storm began to build somewhere deep within him. The realization came crashing through. The last thing he had of Svana was gone.

He'd failed her yet again. Guilt he had been fleeing from every day rammed him and smashed him.

And he bled.

"You," he rumbled.

Cathy swallowed visibly.

"All of this is because of *you!*"

"Andor, I'm so sorry—"

"The defeat, the raven banner, Ubba's death—and now this. You lost the last thing I have from Svana."

She took a step back, horror written all over her face.

"If you were a man," he said, his voice low, "you would lie unconscious right now."

He clenched his fists. The only way he knew how to deal with the devastating emptiness, with the voices building up behind the closed door inside of him, was to distract himself and be on the move.

"But I should not worry. Without Dragon's Trouble—without any weapon—I expect we will both be dead soon. Let us be on our way."

CATHY CHEWED the chunk of stale bread Aethelred had given her. He had also given them warm clothes, including winter cloaks; travel pouches; and more food. She watched Andor's grim face as he stared at the fire, flames dancing in eyes that looked like indigo skies in the darkness of the woods surrounding them. He feasted on a hare he had caught earlier, and Cathy was almost jealous as she inhaled the scent of freshly grilled meat.

Guilt pressed on her shoulders. If someone had lost Brad's surfboard, she'd be devastated. She had only abandoned the wetsuit he'd gotten her because she needed to survive and save Andor's life.

Andor's face was ashen, pain thundering behind his eyes. He didn't say another word to her on their way north. Not that she tried to make him talk. He honored their agreement, even though the sword was not where she had hidden it, and she respected him for it. His face was ashen and pain thundered behind his eyes. Clearly he still hadn't come to terms with his wife's death. What had happened to her? Did he still love her?

She could hardly imagine that this bitter, almost cruel man cared about someone. Surely he was just an arrogant, selfish jerk. Wasn't he?

She continued to study his gorgeous face, so familiar and yet so distant. The golden hair, the beautiful blue eyes, the straight line of the nose that made him look like a proud warrior-king. His lips pressed into a sad, bitter line that cut through his short beard.

He was so handsome. But how could she have ever confused him with Brad? A completely different person shone through him.

She looked down his body. Broad, muscular shoulders under his winter cloak. Would his pecs feel hard under her fingers if she put her hands on them and traced down them? Would his stomach be ripped? Would his skin be smooth? Did he have a lot of hair?

"You are doing it again," he said.

"Hmm?" Cathy's eyes darted away. Her cheeks burned as though he had just caught her red-handed.

"Staring at me. Stop it."

"Oh. Sorry." Her mouth dried.

It was the first thing he'd said to her since they'd left the beach, and she wanted to make peace with him. She needed to know he would forgive her. She stood, moved next to him, and sat down by his side.

He frowned. "What are you doing?"

"I just thought we could talk."

"Talk?"

"Yes. Tell me about yourself."

He rolled his eyes and continued staring at the fire. "Leave me alone."

Ouch. "What can I do to make it okay? So that you forgive me?"

"Disappear," he mumbled.

The words slashed. Even in the Middle Ages she was rejected. "Well, I can't, okay? I have to get back to Brad." Her eyes burned. "As soon as I meet that witch in York, consider me gone."

"At least you have someone to go back to."

"Chances of that are diminishing daily."

He hemmed.

Cathy glanced at him. She'd try again. "So, where do you live? In a castle or something?"

He frowned as if he'd just smelled something bad. "A castle? Of course not. I am no Saxon."

"Right. Then where?"

He sighed. "No more questions, Cathy."

She nodded slowly and pursed her lips, thinking. But she was really curious. And she couldn't stand the silence. Then she remembered. "Wait, if you're a Viking, you live in a wooden house, right?"

"*I* do not."

"Where, then?"

"Nowhere. Stop the questioning."

"Sorry. I'm just curious how things work in this century. Do you have a farm? Or are you some sort of a king? Oh, no, I know—a mercenary?"

Then things got out of control.

He spun to her in a split second, grabbed her by the arm and pulled her to him.

"Enough with your questions," he said in her face. "I swear to Odin, I have never met any woman so...so..."

The touch of his hand, though strong, sent a wave of warmth through her. Inside her veins, fire seethed as his scent reached her—leather and iron and something earthy, something that turned her skin into a gathering of hot, waiting, needing nerve endings. As though he felt the same, the anger in his eyes began turning into something else.

His mouth came closer; there was nothing more she wanted more than to kiss him.

"'Woman so'...what?" she whispered.

"Oh, just shut up."

He wrapped one arm around her waist, pulling her even tighter against him, his other hand cupping the back of her head, igniting the skin on her neck. His mouth claimed hers, overwhelming her with the sensation of his soft lips, his beard pleasantly scratched her skin and propelled her excitement. When her lips parted, he dipped his tongue and began licking and stroking. He wasn't tender or gentle. There was something resembling desperation in his intensity. But when his hand went under her ass, lifting her into his lap, so that her legs straddled him, Cathy stopped.

Brad liked to do that.

Brad.

What am I doing?

She shoved against his chest and jumped up.

And met the confused, furious eyes of an aroused Viking who looked at her like a predator studied his prey.

CHAPTER EIGHT

Andor had never tasted anything as good as Cathy's lips, never smelled anything as delicious as her—roses and the crispness of winter, and the softness of a woman.

When he touched her, it was as though a small lightning bolt crackled where their skin met. The sight of her soft pink lips brought the urge to taste them in a thick, ravenous wave. But there was more. She cared about him, asked questions, wanted to know him better, and a part of him responded. The part that hungered for something deeper, something he had had with Svana and lost forever.

But she had withdrawn, thinking of another man.

And Andor had never felt so rejected.

"Just go to sleep," he mumbled, his veins still hot from the searing desire.

She stood, towering above him, her big gray eyes wide, angry, and confused, heat storming in them.

"Andor, my fiancé—"

"Clearly this was a mistake. It will not happen again. Just

go to sleep. I shall keep watch, then I will wake you and you shall take over."

He turned away from her and wrapped his cloak tighter around himself, ignoring the way her mouth opened as though she was about to say something. She stood still for a moment before moving away from him. Dry leaves rustled under her feet as she walked to the other side of the fire. Andor watched from under his eyelashes as she lay down on the ground and huddled into her cloak. She bent her arm, rested her head on her elbow, then stared at the dying fire, her eyes still wide.

To all the trolls of all the rotten woods—what had possessed him to kiss her? Yes, she was beautiful and very desirable with her tall, curvy, strong body and things to grab in all the right places.

But it was one thing to desire a woman and another to feel something more. He'd had his share of women—meaningless encounters, just to run away from his memories and satisfy the call of the flesh. He had never felt guilty about being with any of them.

He had thought to do the same with Cathy—distract himself, make her shut up. And, well, she was beautiful.

But there had been something more in that kiss. It had felt too good, too delicious. It was as if his mind had blacked out, giving way to something deeper and wider and more intense than he had even felt with Svana.

Something strange.

Something he refused to define. Guilt stung him and the betrayal of Svana's memory echoed in his soul.

He wouldn't allow this any longer. He could not allow himself to care about her because he could not protect those he loved. And he would not be able to endure another loss. The ghosts behind the closed door in his heart made sure to remind him of that. Eyes on the road, eyes towards Jorvik.

The next day they continued on, both of them trying to pretend nothing had happened. Due to his bad leg, he had to make longer stops than he would have liked, but walking was getting easier, although he still needed the stick.

During the first long stop, Andor needed to start a fire to warm them. He twirled the small stick he had carved earlier between his hands, pressing it against a hearth-board, next to the notch he had cut into one side. The friction produced charred sawdust.

Cathy watched him with an open mouth.

"Something interesting you are seeing?" he said.

"Sorry, I'm staring. Can I help?"

"You could have helped by not losing my belt pouch. There was a fire-steel. Had I it now, the campfire would already be warming your tired feet."

Cathy rolled her eyes. "Well. Sorry for saving your life. Can I do something now?"

Andor eyed her. "Can you start a fire?"

"No."

"Then you can learn. I am not going to do this every time. Come here."

Cathy sat next to him by the hearth-board. The scent of her, flowery and crisp, tickled his nostrils, igniting something hot and predatory in his stomach. He exhaled, chasing the hunger away. It was just a normal male reaction to an attractive woman. A woman he would not touch.

He returned to the stick and twirled it between his palms. "I must twirl it until coal forms from the hearth-board wood and drops onto the dry leaves and sticks below. The hardest part is to twirl and press downward at the same time. If both of us work at it, we can do it faster."

Cathy nodded. "Sure. Do you want me to twirl or to press?"

I want you to do both, gently, and not to this stick.

Loki. Andor suppressed a groan.

"Press," he said. "Take a flat piece of rock, like that one." He nodded towards one lying nearby. "Press against the stick with your weight while I do the twirling."

"Okay," Cathy said.

She picked up the rock and positioned it on top of the stick, her head bent over it, close to Andor's. He could see her beautiful face, her scent reaching him. He held his breath for a moment, then cursed inwardly and returned his attention to the stick.

He began twirling, and it was much easier with Cathy's help. Soon, the dark sawdust began falling through the notch onto the dry leaves. He moved his hands, fast, and the wood was giving in, blackening under the spindle. Cathy's presence next to him was sweet and distracting. He realized that they had begun breathing in one rhythm, and he coughed, uncomfortable from the warmth of her nearness. His palms ached and his hands were tired when coals finally fell on the tinder and it began smoking.

Andor stopped the twirling and signaled for Cathy to get back, which brought relief but also a protest. He lowered himself towards the tinder, which lay on a piece of wood, and blew on it gently. Fire sparkled and caught, and he carried it over to a small arrangement of kindling, brushwood, and firewood.

When the scorching tinder landed there, fire caught, and Andor blew some more until he was sure the fire would not be extinguished by the wind. When it burned strong and warm, he looked at Cathy, who watched him with an expression of wonder.

"Next time, you will twirl," he said to chase away the warmth that the look planted inside of him.

DURING THE NEXT THREE DAYS, Andor and Cathy fell into a sort of routine. They found a trail that led them in the right direction and followed it. Being careful, they hid behind trees whenever they heard the pounding of hooves or saw anyone in the distance. They passed by woods and swamps and rolling hills. Snow fell only once, covering the ground in a gentle white dusting.

Cathy stopped her questions and stopped staring at him as if she were seeing a living ghost, but Andor found himself staring at her more often that he liked.

When she was not hounding him with questions, she was a good road companion.

"Gather brushwood for the fire," he would say when they found a place to stay for the night.

"Sure," she would answer and walk into the woods.

"I can take the first watch and wake you up in a couple of hours," she would offer after dinner.

Even after a long day of walking she did not complain of being tired, although he could see the dark circles under her eyes.

A familiar warmth of companionship settled in his chest, the same feeling he had when he was on the road with his loyal sword-brothers.

Thankfully, they did not say much apart from if they needed to stop or who would gather firewood and who would keep watch.

Andor did not know how she could still walk after eating only stale bread while he feasted on grilled hares and fowls.

On the third morning, Cathy woke up and looked into her purse then closed it with a concerned look. "I'm out of bread. What can I forage in winter that's edible?"

Andor chuckled. "Hare," he said and offered her the leg he had grilled last night.

She looked at it with longing but shook her head. "No. There must be something else."

"Maiden, winter is not a good time to be picky in the wilderness."

Her stomach grumbled loudly, and she grimaced.

"Your body agrees," he said.

"Well, my body is only one part of the system. My spirit will thank it later. I haven't done yoga for what feels like a thousand years." She sniffed under her tunic and wrinkled her nose. "God, I'd do anything for a hot shower," she mumbled to herself. "I'm going to go into the woods and do yoga, okay?"

He frowned at first, not entirely sure what her words meant, then he remembered that yoga was some sort of training she taught.

"Do not go far," he said.

She raised her eyebrows, and Andor realized he had slipped.

"If you get attacked, I do not want to have to waste time looking for your body before resuming the journey," he explained, although he winced internally at the cruelness of his own words.

She rolled her eyes and walked away.

Andor had to admit, he was curious about that "yoga." When he finished his breakfast, he decided to watch her do it. Maybe it would shed some light on where the madwoman had really come from and why she was lying to him.

He followed her tracks down the slope as softly as he could manage with his bad leg. The burbling of water met his ears soon, and after a while he saw Cathy by a stream.

She was, indeed, doing something. Her cloak lay next to her on the ground, and she did a series of movements that resembled— The closest thing he could think of was a witch's dance. She glided from position to position, every movement precise and graceful, as though she drew runes in the air with her body. Body straight, arms up in the air, then down, touching the ground so that her legs and her torso came together in two lines. How did she manage to keep her legs so straight? Then up again, with her arms wide like the wings of a bird—then shooting them into the sky like two spears.

She went on, lowering herself, stretching her legs, crouching, over and over again in a mesmerizing flux. She flowed and yet her muscles were toned and energized. Andor lost himself watching her. Calmness he had not felt in a long time enveloped him.

The last time he had experienced it was when Svana had been alive and she had lain in his arms in their bed.

Too soon, Cathy stopped and sat on the ground with her legs crossed, her palms together in front of her chest, eyes closed. Andor watched her sit like this for a long time. When she finally opened her eyes, her face was so calm and so relaxed, joyous even, that he felt a sting of jealousy.

Joy like that was not possible for him.

He was about to turn around and walk back to the fire when she began undressing herself.

She undid the belt and pulled the tunic over her head. Underneath it was something he had never seen before—some sort of black undergarment that clung to her like a second skin, highlighting every curve.

Then off came the baggy trousers and she was left in a smaller black undergarment that reminded him of very short trousers, which hugged her thighs. She removed the shoes, too, and then the woolen socks, and stood before the stream, steam rising slowly and rhythmically from her mouth.

It was a warm day but still the middle of winter, and he admired Cathy's readiness to enter the icy cold water.

If he thought she looked beautiful with a man's baggy clothes on, now with almost nothing to cover her body, she took Andor's breath away. Long legs, a thin waist, beautiful curved hips, a gorgeous round arse that made his hands itch to grab and massage it. Full breasts just the right size and form to make a man forget everything else around him.

Then she removed the top and he saw the soft side of her breast. Off came her short trousers, and the sight of her naked behind woke an animal-like need within him. Her body was both sculpted and soft. Beneath the curves were clearly strong muscles. Her skin was flawless, and it looked like it would be the softest thing he'd ever touched. The sight both tortured and pleased him, and his eyes stayed glued to her.

She let her hair fall loose down her back before moving towards the water. Without a peep, she walked into the slow flowing stream. She went completely under, then emerged and began washing herself. This was what a goddess or a Valkyrie or a princess must look like. Beautiful, graceful, peaceful, like a part of nature itself.

Andor watched, enthralled.

Soon, she turned back and moved towards the grassy bank, and Andor forgot to hide behind a tree. Their eyes locked, and time stood still. The water only came up to the middle of her thighs. The skin of her breasts, stomach, and hips were reddened from cold. He became aware of his hot, swelling erection but could do nothing about it.

Her eyes widened in surprise, her face pink from embarrassment. Surprisingly, she did not cover herself. But whatever she was thinking right now, there was no rejection in her eyes or her face. In fact, her lips parted, her nipples hardened even more, and her gray eyes darkened.

If he took one more step towards her, they would come together, right here, right now.

Both of them waited for the other to move.

No.

Andor could not. Should not. If he started anything with her, he would want to protect her, and what if he was not able to?

Not for a second time.

He swallowed. With an effort equal to pulling a whale from the sea, he turned around and left.

CHAPTER NINE

"That *yoga* you were doing," Andor said as they continued north through the woods. "Is it a dance?"

Cathy glanced at him, surprised. This was the softest voice he had ever used with her.

"Did you see me do yoga, too?" she asked.

The memory of him staring at her naked body sent her pulse racing.

Earlier this morning, it had felt so good to do her yoga routine again, to calm her mind, to connect to her body. Afterwards, washing in the stream, even if her skin ached from the cold, was so invigorating, so refreshing that for the first time since she'd arrived in this time—maybe even since Brad's accident—she felt strong, she felt like herself.

She'd even asked herself if she really needed that jerk, Andor, to find the way to York.

Bliss had evaporated when she'd seen him watching her. The heat in his eyes could have boiled the icy water in the stream. It had certainly set *her* blood simmering. Her knees had gone weak and her heart had pumped harder and her mouth had dried. The world had stood still as their eyes locked. If either of them had lifted a finger, the air between them would have crackled like a ball of lightning.

No one had looked at her that way—ever.

Not even Brad.

"I saw you," Andor said. "I have never seen anything like what you were doing."

Her cheeks were warming, a smile threatening to appear on her face.

Oh, what was wrong with her? She was *enjoying* the attention of this arrogant Viking.

Stupid, pathetic, and needy. A little male attention, and she was ready to swoon. She had Brad to think about, the only man who loved her and whom she loved.

Get your shit together, you wimp. You cannot start developing feelings for a Viking only because he saw you naked and seemed to like it.

"Well," she said, "you haven't seen it because you guys have probably not even heard of India yet. But in the future, the whole world is connected. Globalization brings everything together. Japanese sushi, clothes made in China, French wine available in every supermarket. So yoga has become popular all around the world."

Andor hemmed, clearly confused.

"Why? Did you want to try?" she said.

"Try?" he laughed. "No. I do not dance."

Typical man.

"It's not a dance, Andor. It could only do you good. Calm you down. Maybe even help your leg heal a little faster."

He shook his head. "It reminded me of a völva I've seen who was doing a dance by the fire to connect to the gods. But hers was wild and chaotic. Yours—it was different. There was no chaos in it. It brought—"

He stopped talking, as if searching for words.

"Peace?" Cathy said.

"Yes. Peace. Peace spread through me from just looking at you."

Cathy smiled. "Yes. Yoga can do that."

Andor chuckled. "I forgot what peace was."

Cathy frowned. She shouldn't be surprised. The life of a Viking warrior wasn't all feasts and sailing. But there was something in his voice that made her think there was more to it for him. He was tormented.

Andor continued. "It seemed like magic to me, what you were doing. Like a spell. How else could I suddenly feel peaceful like that, just by looking at you?"

It wasn't a direct compliment, but his voice rang with approval, respect—and even wonder. All for her—from a man like him. Her stomach filled with lightness, a smile spread on her lips, something Brad brought out in her. Except, Brad had never said a mean word to her, whereas Andor's previous disapproval made his words even more meaningful. Though she knew how messed up that was, she couldn't help the warmth spreading in her stomach and chest.

She felt lightheaded.

Maybe she was just hungry.

"So, you don't think I'm crazy?" she said.

Andor paused for a moment beside a large bush, his eyes on her. "No. I do not think you are mad."

Relief flooded Cathy, and her smile grew.

"And even if you are," he added, "a part of me wants to be mad like that. If that would mean I would get even a drop of your peace."

Cathy's eyes prickled. The intoxication of being approved of made every cell ring like a yoga gong. Was it even true what he was saying?

"Well—" she began, but Andor turned to look somewhere to her right.

"This is a hazelnut tree," he said. "Can you eat nuts?"

Cathy glanced at the tall bush with bare branches and saw small nuts on them.

"Yes," she said. "Oh, thank you, yes."

She launched at the bush and picked the nuts. She found a rock, smashed the nuts one by one. With trembling fingers, she cleaned the nuts from the shells as best she could and began sticking them into her mouth. She'd had no idea how hungry she was until now. They tasted earthy and were cold and a little dry, but after almost a week on nothing but bread and water, they tasted divine. Plus, they were organic. How often did she get to eat real forest nuts back in her time?

Andor watched her with an amused smile. "Freyja and Frigg, watching you, they look like they taste as sweet as mead from Valhalla. Give me one."

She threw one to him and he chewed it, then spat. "These taste like dust."

"Shut up," she said, her mouth full. "They do not."

"Not as juicy as a grilled hare."

She rolled her eyes. After she was somewhat full, Cathy picked all the nuts she could find and stored them in the travel pouch. There was another bush next to the first one and she did the same there. It wasn't much, maybe enough food to last a day or two if she ate them sparingly.

"If you see any more on the way, let me know," she said, patting the purse.

As they turned to continue, Andor went still beside her. Leaves rustled, and Cathy saw two men approaching through the woods. One had a long knife, the other one an ax.

Her skin crawled. The trouble had begun much sooner than she'd thought it would.

She glanced at Andor, but he looked as if he was quickly assessing the situation.

He had nothing but a kitchen knife he had stolen from the monastery—the only weapon Cathy and he could find there. It had come in handy to slaughter the hares and dress them for a roast, but surely that was not great compared to a sword or a battle ax.

Oh god, and what about his wound?

The men wore what looked like rags, and she doubted they were trained warriors. Maybe just desperate farmers or crafts-men. Cathy hoped they just thought Andor was a cripple with a stick, which he was likely going to use as a weapon, and that Cathy looked like an overgrown teenage boy.

"Not a word," Cathy mumbled, her eyes on the men. "You are a mute, remember?"

Andor didn't answer, just eyed them like a hawk.

The men stopped in front of them—one was short and stout, the other a head taller and lean as a tree branch.

"Hullo," the shorter one said, his knife gripped tightly.

"I think you know what is about to happen," the other one said, laying the handle of his ax on the palm of his other hand.

Cathy swallowed. "We don't have anything."

The first one looked her over, head to toe, and narrowed his eyes. She noticed Andor's muscles tense.

"Looking at you, I suppose that is true enough," the first bandit said. "But I do like your cloak. It looks so much warmer than my jacket."

He wore a quilted jacket with holes in it. "And those boots." He looked down at her feet, and she noted his boots were much more worn-out.

"Look," she said, the familiar terror of being bullied grip-ping her whole body. "Just go on your way. We don't want trouble."

The taller man squinted at her. "What's your name, boy?" he said.

Cathy cleared her throat, remembering to lower her voice. "Cathan."

The taller man's face straightened, a sly smile spreading in his shaggy beard.

"You know what, Basil, I do not think 'tis a Cathan at all." With his ax ready, he walked to Cathy.

He approached her, his face dirty and his mouth gaping with black spaces from missing teeth. Her stomach cold with fear, she took several steps back.

"I think it's a wo—"

A cloak and blond hair flashed before her, and the man was on the ground, clutching at his bleeding throat. The short man ran, but Andor took the tall man's ax and threw it at him. The man fell with the ax stuck in his back.

Cathy pushed down a scream, her hands pressed to her mouth. The contents of her stomach rose, and only the thought that if she vomited now she would likely starve kept her from giving in to the impulse.

Andor turned to her, the bloody kitchen knife in one hand. His eyebrows rose and one side of his mouth curled up. "You look like you are about to shit yourself, *Cathan*. I thought you were a warrior."

She frowned and removed her hands from her mouth. "I told you, I'm not a warrior."

"No?" He walked towards the man with the ax in his back. "Maybe you should be."

CHAPTER TEN

"Thank you for saving me," Cathy said when they resumed walking.

Andor gritted his teeth, his gut still churning with battle fury. "I did not save you."

"You did."

"I told you, do not hold me responsible for your life. I merely chose the best moment to act given my disadvantage in weapons. He was distracted by you. I would not have had a better opportunity."

She stopped and faced him, forcing him to stop, too. "Oh, like if he had reached me, you wouldn't have done anything. You'd just watch him"—she paused—"do whatever he was about to do to me..."

"Do not read anything more into it than there is."

Cathy scoffed. "I'm just saying—I think you are a better person than you want me to believe."

Andor was beginning to lose his patience. "I do not want you to believe anything. I care not if you think me a good person or Loki's spawn. I stopped the two bandits because they had to be stopped. Your well-being had little to do with it."

But a tiny voice in him whispered that it had been more than a good moment to act and more than the practicality of having her as his companion.

When the bastard had almost reached her, Andor's body had reacted like an arrow launched from an overstretched bow. She had been in danger, and fear for her had twisted his gut. The need to protect her had risen in him like a surging storm he could not stop. He could not stand by and watch her get hurt, could not have the same thing happen to her that had happened to Svana. He could not fail a second time.

And he hated feeling compelled to protect her, knowing he could not succeed. Knowing he could not live with the guilt of failure.

He must will himself to fight the impulse.

Maybe he should stop looking at her, asking her about yoga, helping her find food.

Cathy resumed walking. "A little human connection and you ruffle like a hedgehog. Why are you so defensive? Is it a Viking thing?"

Andor followed her, watching her cloak moving in front of him, his gut tense. Her words tapped on the wrong door, the one where all of the painful memories were locked away.

And those memories began tapping back.

He remembered the first time he had seen Svana. Andor had just become the jarl after his father's death and had been looking for a wife. He should have married another jarl's daughter to strengthen alliances, but when he had visited her father Harek's feast in the new jarl's honor, Svana had beguiled Andor. He had been cocky, and he'd wanted her. "I will earn the respect of other jarls through my actions, not by marrying someone's daughter," Andor had told Fridstein. "I must marry this one."

She'd loved him and she'd married him. Look where it had gotten her.

The memory of Svana's gaping wound, her weak voice, the feel of her warm, soft body in his arms...

Cathy's voice brought him back, releasing him from the prison of his memories. "Seriously, though?" she said. "What happened to you that made you like this?"

He knew he should not venture there. But before he could stop himself, the words blurted out. "Like what?" He winced. "Forget it," he said.

"No, no. Don't forget it. I'll tell you. You behave as though caring about someone is a weakness."

Andor staggered as if he had just hit an invisible wall. "Do not talk about things that you do not know, woman."

"You're right. I don't know. That's why I'm asking. Do you have a family? Parents? What happened to your wife?"

Her words lashed him, cutting deep.

"I lost her," he snarled.

Cathy stopped. "How?"

Too much. Darkness was swallowing him.

He saw flames licking the walls of his village, life fading from her eyes, then more flames consuming her body as the funeral boat floated silently away, taking his heart with it.

Run! Run! Run!

"No. I shall not talk of her with you."

"It might actually help to talk—"

"Enough!" he barked, and Cathy jerked. "I do *not* need to talk about her. About me. Or about you."

She lowered her eyes. "Sorry."

"We should probably go our separate ways."

"No. Please, Andor. I'm sorry. I'll shut up. I won't say a

word. I must get to York as soon as possible. I'm chatty when I'm nervous, and well—everything that has happened since I arrived here has been crazy. Please, let me come with you. I won't ask again. You're right, it's none of my business."

Andor stared at her. He should leave her. He had two weapons now—the ax and the scramasax. They didn't make up for losing Dragon's Trouble, but they were better than a kitchen knife. If she was going to be as annoying as she was now, no amount of interpreting skills would be worth dragging her with him. He should just say no. He should leave her. But he couldn't bring himself to.

"All right," he said. "If you swear."

"I swear!"

"No. Give me a word on something important. Swear to yoga."

She looked at him with a blank face, then her lips curled a little and a burst of laughter escaped her lips. "I'm so sorry, but what you just said, it's so funny."

Andor ground his teeth. "There is nothing funny about this. Laugh once again and I will leave you behind."

"Okay, okay. I won't laugh."

"What do you swear on?"

Her face straightened. She took a deep breath. "On Brad's life. He is the most important person to me."

Her fiancé. The thought of the man she belonged to pained him. And why was his life in danger without Cathy? She had said something about his parents wanting to kill him, but that couldn't be right. And how would Cathy be able to protect him?

No. No asking about her business.

He nodded. "Fine. Let us go." He turned and started walking, then his eyes fell on white mushrooms growing on the bark of a tree. He pointed. "You can eat those."

Cathy frowned at them, dubious. "Really?"

Andor sighed. "Yes. Really."

Cathy raised her brows and cocked her head to the side. A slow smile spread across her face. "Something other than bread and nuts—Andor, I'm going to feast tonight."

Joy burst in him at the sight of Cathy happily picking the mushrooms. He cursed. The woman was getting under his skin.

But he just could not resist seeing her pleased.

Thor's stinky feet. Andor was in trouble.

CATHY'S *smooth skin glowed in the dancing light of the campfire. The gentle arch of her waist, the ripe breasts, the soft curve of her belly loomed over him. They were home, in Hvaldalen, in his bedchamber.*

She straddled him, Andor's cock tightened and swelled inside her. Her golden hair spilled over her sculpted shoulders, covering the top of her breasts. Her moans filled the room as he traced his palm from her stomach up between her breasts then cupped one and circled her nipple with his thumb until it hardened.

She rode him, her eyes closed. Her head fell back, exposing her beautiful neck.

"Andor," she moaned. "Andor..."

"Yes, my beauty. Enjoy the ride."

He took both her breasts in his hands and massaged them, making her clench around him tighter.

"Oh, Andor, why were you late?" she moaned, still gliding on top of him.

He froze. "What?"

"Why were you late? You promised you would be back a moon ago."

He rose on his elbows, an icy cold spear stuck in his throat.

"I did not promise you anything, Cathy. I told you from the start, I will not be responsible for you."

She stopped moving and opened her eyes. They were green. The smell of burning wood and the iron tang of blood filled his nostrils.

"You promised," she said.

Andor blinked. It was not Cathy. It was Svana, her hair not golden anymore but brown. Her side gaped with a deep wound.

The granite torc around his neck grew heavier. People screamed in pain, metal rang against metal.

"I am sorry, Svana."

Fire rose around their bed. The walls became charcoal, and heavy, wet smoke filled the room.

"You promised. Had you come on time—"

"I am sorry!" he yelled as the fire consumed the bed.

"Andor," someone called. "Andor."

Everything shook, as though a giant stomped on the ground.

"Wake up, Andor."

He opened his eyes. Fire lit Cathy's worried face above him, dark against the night. She shook him by the shoulder. The scent of a forest, rotting leaves and wet earth, hit him. An owl hooted. Branches rustled in the wind.

He jerked to sit upright, tugging the cloak to cover his erection. Odin and Thor, he was still aroused after the dream. He still wanted Cathy, despite the horror of everything else he had seen.

"It was just a dream," she said. "You're okay. Nothing is chasing you."

He breathed heavily, his chest tight with the echo of the memories.

"You are wrong about that," he croaked. "Go to sleep. I am awake now. I shall do the night watch."

"Are you sure? You barely slept."

"I will not sleep even if I try."

As she lay on the ground, huddled in her cloak by the fire, he thought that she was very wrong about nothing chasing him.

The ghosts were. The more he wanted Cathy, the more they haunted him.

And he still could not stop wanting her.

But he had to try.

CHAPTER ELEVEN

Lands near Ashbury, Oxfordshire, January 18, 878 AD

For the past three days, all Cathy had seen were trees, the rolling hills of the English—or Wessex—countryside, and Andor's stern profile as they walked side by side up the road to the northeast. The leaden winter sky and bare forests were the perfect mirror of her mood.

Whatever signs of admiration and appreciation Andor had showed Cathy before were only in her head. He had made it clear that she should stay away. "We should probably go our separate ways," he had said. He didn't want anything to do with her. Maybe he had just been surprised to see her naked and had reacted the way any man would to a naked woman. And she had read too much into it.

Cathy looked down at her boots moving on the damp packed-earth road. Her vision blurred and her eyes began burning.

In his rough woolen cloak, with an ax and a long dagger,

Andor seemed to her as much a part of the dark, brooding landscape as the solemn trees on either side.

Whereas she… Even without the hot-pink wetsuit, she felt like an outsider, a tourist, as though the very woods and sky frowned at her.

She had kept her promise and not asked any more questions about his personal life, though they burned on her tongue. She forced herself to swallow them, just like she swallowed her words when her mom told her that she chatted way too much and that she already stood out with her height and weight.

Mostly, she and Andor walked in silence.

Every morning, Cathy walked away from their little camp to do yoga. Not too far though, so that Andor could come watch her if he wanted to. But because of that, she could never really get into it.

Secretly, she wanted for him to join her. One, yoga would do him good. Something haunted him, and Cathy firmly believed yoga and meditation could bring him relief. Two, pathetically, embarrassingly, and despite his rejection, she craved his attention. His approval and his compliments had intoxicated her. She wanted more.

But he never came.

Later that evening, while they were setting up camp, she couldn't keep her anxiety over his opinion of her down anymore.

Andor was crouching in front of the fire, stoking it.

"Look, Andor," she said, and he turned his head towards her, his face pinched in silent warning.

Oh no. She should stop.

She couldn't.

"I was thinking… You should come with me tomorrow morning to do yoga."

He narrowed his eyes at her. "What? Where does this come from?"

"Well, I just—I know you were curious, earlier. You were asking me about it. Would you like to try?"

"You've just broken your word."

"Come on, you can't seriously expect me to not talk to you for the rest of this journey."

He shook his head and returned to his work. "Leave me alone."

She could help him get through this. She just needed him to see. "You clearly have anger issues—issues about caring. Your heart—"

He jumped to his feet, his eyes a mixture of anguish and fury. "Woman, I am warning you, one more word and you shall be sorry."

His voice was so thick and full of threat, Cathy shrank.

"How is it possible that I'm trying to help you, and all you give me is anger and hatred?"

Andor straightened up, his chest rising and falling, his eyes wide under his furrowed brows. "Because you are constantly disturbing my peace."

"Peace? You have no peace."

"Yes, I do. I did. Maybe not peace like you, but my own version of peace. When I do not need to watch over annoying females."

"I don't need to be watched over."

"I thought you said you needed me."

"Only because you know the way."

"I do not know the way."

"Well. You know how to orient by the sun or whatever. I can hardly find my way using maps on my phone."

"For Odin and Thor. There is nothing to orient. Follow this road. It goes north." He sliced a hand through the air in the direction of the road, which was behind Cathy. "If you are lost, ask someone. You speak the language."

She crossed her arms over her chest. A kernel of stubbornness screamed for her to say, *Fine, I'll go without you.* But how could she leave him alone in enemy territory with his bad leg? She couldn't because she wasn't cruel...and part of her didn't want to leave him. She studied him for any sign that he didn't mean what he said, that it was just his defense mechanism. But all she saw was a gorgeous, furious man who had no interest in her whatsoever. A man who wanted to be left alone.

The story of her life, with the lucky exception of Brad.

Her eyes prickled. "Fine," she said. "Ungrateful man. No 'Thank you, Cathy, for saving me.' No 'Thank you, monks, for treating my wounds.' No 'Sorry I raided your monastery and stole your treasures.' I'm better off without you anyway. It was nice to meet you."

His shoulders slumped in what looked like relief. She picked up her bag, turned away, and walked towards the road through the dusky woods. Her heart was bleeding, her chest aching, her eyes filling with tears. She turned back to see if he was following her.

Silly her.

Of course he wasn't. Why would he?

She sped up and, when she found the road, set into a jog. She wiped her eyes, but the tears kept coming.

She had no idea how long she'd run, but after a while, her tears stopped. Her head ached, and the stupid cap made her scalp itch, so she removed it and shoved it into the bag. It was dark now, and she was exhausted. She needed to stop and rest.

She looked around, but everything looked the same—dark-gray trees and bushes, blackness behind them even under the moonlight.

Except...was that a light glowing between trunks? She stopped and squinted, trying to see.

Wind rustled the trees. Did she hear voices?

Maybe it was a village or a farm or something? Maybe she could spend the night there.

God, what she would give for a proper bed and a blanket. Hell, just sleeping under a roof would be amazing. It would be good for Andor...

Ah well. Screw him. She was on her own now.

Maybe whoever it was had food. She'd finished her mushrooms and nuts some time ago. Her stomach rumbled.

She went through the woods towards the light, stepping as quietly as she could. The closer she got, the louder the voices grew. People talked quietly and hummed some sort of a melody.

Could it be a festival?

It was a small crowd, maybe twenty people standing in a circle and three by what looked like a tall, flat rock. Like a table. The light came from several campfires and from torches in people's hands. Among them stood several horses.

Behind them was a small hill with giant rocks standing like columns. Leaning against the hill was a large, almost-round rock that bore a chalk drawing of a horse. Right under the rock, a campfire burned, making the chalk horse move in the dancing flames.

A man in a long robe and a heavy apron stood by the table. The top glistened with something dark. Fear knotted Cathy's stomach. Could it be blood? Two dead goats lay next to the table, and on it, she suddenly realized, was a third one, still alive. Cathy's feet chilled, her pulse racing. Poor animals! The man wore a metal band on his head with engraving along its length. His hands held a butcher's knife high above the goat.

The animal struggled in the hands of two men who held it by its legs.

Cathy's skin crawled as she began to understand what she had walked into.

A pagan sacrifice.

"Wēland, the invisible smith! Take this silver coin and take this sacrifice in your honor. Repair our weapons, chain mail and horseshoes, and armor us against Danes, so that our land is finally free of them."

The woods began closing in around her. Her arms and legs grew weak, and she began hyperventilating. A scream rose in her throat, but she covered her mouth and stopped it. She needed to get out of here. Why had she left Andor? She was such a fool to think she could make it all the way to York without running into trouble.

The priest's hands fell, and with one swift motion he cut off the goat's head, ending its cries and sending blood gushing forth.

Cathy yelped in horror even through her cold fingers.

While another man held a bowl under the altar and gathered blood, several people looked in her direction. And one man saw her and narrowed his eyes.

Horror paralyzed Cathy. She couldn't move a digit, her breath caught as though in a steel vise. Everything within her screamed at her to run, but she could only watch him and four more men and women coming right at her. They were just a few steps away when she finally unfroze, turned, and ran.

But she might as well have been in a nightmare. She moved way too slow, as if she was slogging through a swamp. She willed her legs to pump faster, but the pagans were right behind her. They grasped her hands, and someone knocked her to the ground.

A man with bad breath pointed a knife right at her throat.

"Who are you?" he said in Old English.

The rest of them loomed over her, their faces dark against the light of the fires behind their backs.

Cathy shook. She needed to lie.

"I'm from your village," she said, trying to make her voice low, like a boy's. "I'm Katherine's son, remember?"

The man's face straightened, and a sly smile spread on his face.

"I have no village, there is no Katherine, and you are no boy." He looked up at his companions. "We are lucky. Today, we feed the smith-god a woman."

CHAPTER TWELVE

ANDOR GROANED as the Saxon pagans dragged Cathy towards the sacrifice mound.

He recognized a blot. Before Christianity had infested the kingdoms of Bretland, Saxons, like Norsemen, had believed in the rightful gods. This must be a tribe that still worshiped the old gods. Andor did not understand the language, but he recognized the name Völundr, a talented smith, married to a Valkyrie and enslaved by a king for his skills. Although Völundr the Smith was not a god in the Norse understanding, the pagan Saxons were making a sacrifice to him.

Hidden behind a tree, Andor watched them. He should have come after Cathy sooner. Why had he even hesitated? He had been cruel to her, trying to keep a distance between them. With every moment spent with Cathy, the memory of his wife became weaker, and Cathy's presence stronger, fuller, bigger.

She enriched him with her lightness, her kindness, and her willpower. Even though he thought it was silly that she refused to eat meat while she was clearly hungry, she believed it was not good for her. And her determination showed strength and discipline. She might not be a warrior, but she had a warrior's spirit.

And now she was struggling and screaming, about to be slaughtered, all because of him. The priest listened to Cathy's captor, then nodded. Andor could see his eyes harden in the torch light.

He said something to the struggling Cathy, who began thrashing harder, trying to free herself. Fear for her gripped his gut.

This was exactly what he had been terrified of, running away from: watching someone he cared about die because of his neglect.

He gripped the handle of his ax. There were twenty-three of them, men and women. He was alone. If he had not been wounded and had been fully armed, he would have charged the priest and grabbed her. He might have had a chance.

But not with a bad leg and not without a shield.

He needed to use his cunning.

They tried to lift Cathy onto the altar, but she kicked one in the stomach and broke loose. Using their shock, she ran towards the woods, only to be caught by the onlookers. Someone slapped her hard twice, and she went limp and crumpled to the ground.

Andor's fists clenched, fingernails digging into his flesh.

The only things he had were his cloak, his weapons, and his clothes. Then he noticed the chalk drawings on the stones. Looking around, he saw several white rocks. With chalk dust, he could paint his face white. They wanted Völundr. They would get Völundr.

He picked up a few white stones near his feet—they felt soft in his hand. He bashed them with the pommel of the scramasax, hoping the noise of the crowd would muffle the sound. Then he took handfuls of the white powder and rubbed it over his face. Picking up a small clump of earth from beneath his feet, he spat into his hand and made a dark paste, then rubbed it around his eyes. He quickly drew a white snake on the blade of the scramasax and rubbed the blade of the ax white.

He had no idea if this would work. Maybe they'd see right through him and sacrifice him with Cathy.

But it was better to try and die than to live with another woman's death on his hands.

He was not responsible for her, though. He'd told her that and, therefore, freed himself of the responsibility. He was doing it because he could, he reminded himself. Because he wanted to, not because he had to.

The men were lifting Cathy onto the altar again, and he was out of time. Quickly, he put the hood of his cape up, leaving his face out so that they'd see the white.

Leaving the shelter of the trees, Andor strode towards the crowd. Cathy lay on the altar, the priest with his knife high above her neck. She watched silently, as if the Norn whispered her doom, but then came to her senses and began yelling and struggling.

The priest was saying a prayer, his voice rising, coming to a peak, when Andor stepped into the light and droned "Ahhhhh!"

Everyone turned to him, their eyes widening as they looked him up and down. The priest went silent, looking stunned.

"Ahhhhhhhh!" Andor repeated and pointed with his scramasax at Cathy.

She watched him with terrified eyes.

"Cathy, do as I say," he sang low, on one note.

Her mouth opened. She nodded.

"Tell them, I am Völundr, and I came for my wife, the Valkyrie Hervör, and if they try to stop me, I shall turn all their ironwork into rot and rust."

Cathy swallowed and looked at the priest, then began translating, and the priest's eyes widened in surprise. They needed to use the astonishment of the Saxons to their advantage.

"Move, Cathy," Andor said. Cathy freed her arms from the hands of the men, who let her go.

She jumped off the altar and walked to Andor. The priest said a single word, which made her stop. Then he asked something, and she paled.

"He asks why is it that you do not speak their tongue."

"Helheim. Be ready to run."

He looked at the horses who were grazing peacefully among the people. The beasts were their only chance of escape.

He gestured with the scramasax for the people to make way. They stepped aside, one by one, the crowd moving away from Andor like water under a longship's hull. The priest's eyes burned as he watched Andor walk towards him step by step.

"Tell him that is because I do not wish to speak the same tongue as the man who threatened to kill my wife. If he wants me to help them with ironwork, he must do as I say."

While she translated, Andor hauled himself onto the back of a nearby horse, his true destination. "Tell him I much prefer horses to goats, so I will take this one. Then approach me, slowly."

She did as he asked, and the priest's eyes narrowed. He said something else, his voice rising, as he looked straight at Andor.

"Quick, Cathy," Andor said.

She sprinted. The priest's brows snapped together, his mouth curving downward. People exchanged glances, their shoulders tensing. Andor's heart pounded, and his hands clenched around the reins.

The priest shouted an order, and several people caught at Cathy as she ran, finally stopping her. Andor roared. He took the ax and began hacking. Some of them staggered back, while other men ran towards him with their knives and axes ready. Screams of pain and terror filled the air. "Wēland!" they screamed. "Wēland!"

The last man holding Cathy fell, and she ran to Andor. He held out his hand, and she grabbed his forearm with both hands. He pulled her up, settling her behind him. As more men with weapons ran towards them, he pulled the reins and spurred the horse to a gallop. It flew through the dark woods, along a trail lit only by the moon. Thundering hooves and shouts closed in behind them. He glanced back over his shoulder; the riders followed him.

"Hya!" Andor spurred the horse, his veins throbbing with the rush of it. "Hya!"

If he managed to get them away from their pursuers, they'd have a horse. If, however, the pagans caught them, they would both be dead.

They galloped for some time, but it was hard for their horse to carry two people. Only two riders followed them now. He could fight two.

Ahead, through the trees, stood a huge hill. Even in the darkness of the night, giant, white lines and curves shone from the hillside. What was that? The sight would have made him haul on the reins if he was not being pursued by the enemies. But there was no time for fear or awe. He had to think fast.

If he climbed the hill, he could use the position to his advantage.

"We go there," he yelled to Cathy. "When we are up, I will dismount, and you must go on. Do you hear me?"

"I'm not leaving you!" she said.

"Yes, you are."

They rode to the top of the hill, then stopped, and he jumped down. Cathy did the same.

"I told you—" Andor yelled, but she interrupted.

"To quote you, 'I don't need your help.'"

"Down, now," Andor hissed. From below, their enemies would not be able to see if they were still on the hill, or what their position was.

They were coming, blindly charging up the hill. Andor was ready, and with a trained precision, threw the ax as the first man reached the top. It caught the rider in the chest, and he fell, the beast charging wildly away. Without warning, the second rider crested the hill. He swung at Andor, but Andor moved fast, and the sword grazed off his shoulder, leaving a shallow wound.

The rider galloped further along the hilltop, turned his horse and rode right at Andor. He planted his feet in the soft turf. The man charged at full speed, swinging his sword. It was the priest. Andor held fast as the horse barreled towards him. Then, at the last moment, he ducked under the priest's swing and thrust the scramasax into the man's side. Mouth gaping in a silent cry, the priest pitched off the horse and rolled down the hill as the animal galloped away.

Andor breathed heavily, looking around in case more enemies were on their way. But there were none. Cathy watched him with her soft gray eyes. They locked gazes.

They had won. He had saved her. He had come for her.

And she had stayed for him.

It was as though the air between them was sucked away, as though they were pulled towards each other by an unstoppable force. She flew into his arms, and he crushed her to him.

She was warm and tall, her muscles hard but her curves soft. Her scent hit him—the freshness of the forest and the sweetness of a rose, and her, the womanly, light, seductive scent that was hers alone—and his blood boiled.

He kissed her, sinking into the softness of her lips and the silky pleasure of her tongue. Hunger for her roared through him. He wanted her whole. Like a teenage boy on his first raiding trip, the excitement squeezed his stomach. As a sea of heat sent its waves through him, somewhere deep he knew that he would always want more of these kisses, more of her touch. More of her.

CHAPTER THIRTEEN

ANDOR'S MOUTH DEMANDED, claimed, and yet brushed hers with the softest touches. His arms enveloped her, crushing her to him, pressing her breasts against his hard chest, her nipples hardening and aching sweetly.

She heard a moan born somewhere deep within her rise up. He echoed it and kissed her faster, hungrier. Desire sizzled through her veins and melted her body. Her head spun and her body floated.

More, deeper, these clothes are so restrictive.

Suddenly he broke the kiss, looking towards the woods.

"Did you hear that?" he asked.

"What?" she mumbled, her lips swollen and warm.

"They are coming for us."

Sobering, she glanced at the woods. Lights moved between the trees, and people hollered. There were so many of them, like sparks from a bonfire, and all her arousal evaporated, fear chilling her.

"We must go," he said. "Take a sword and sheath from the

man there. I'll see if I can find the priest's sword." He gestured halfway down the hillside, where the silhouette of a man lay.

Without waiting for her response, he hurried down the hill. "Wait, Andor!" she called after him, but he didn't look back.

All right, Cathy, be strong. Why did this journey have to involve looting dead people?

But, thankfully, she didn't have to do anything too grisly this time, because the sword lay next to the rider in the grass. She found the sheath around the man's waist and unbuckled it, strapping it around her own hips. Then she took the sword in both hands. They sank from the weight, but she lifted the blade up, her muscles singing.

The voices got louder. She put the sword in the sheath and ran to the horse they'd escaped on, grabbing its reins. She had no idea how to deal with a horse, and she was a little afraid of it, not sure what to expect. Even though she had ridden the same animal with Andor just now, she didn't know how to talk to it or make it do what she wanted.

It gazed patiently at her, its large dark eyes fringed with long eyelashes. She clicked her tongue as she'd heard other riders do. "Come on, sweetheart," she said while pulling the reins. And, surprisingly, the horse obeyed. "Good girl."

Cathy brought it to the crest of the hill and glanced down. Andor was already on the way up.

Behind him, people with torches ran up the hill.

His eyes fell on the sheathed sword, and he nodded in approval. Then he scooped her up in his giant arms and set her on the horse, mounting behind her. "Let us go."

They flew, Andor's strong torso against Cathy's back, and the muscles of the horse bunching under her. She looked back as they were about to descend the hill and finally realized what the white lines through the green grass were—an enormous drawing resembling those made by prehistoric people on cave walls. A giant horse.

THEY RODE THE WHOLE NIGHT, and when the horse began tiring, they turned off the road into the woods and continued until they found a stream. Andor let the beast drink and graze while he set about making a fire. Dawn began to break, chasing away the darkness of the night, coloring the trees in dark silver.

When the fire crackled, he sat down and looked at Cathy from behind the flames. It was better there was something between them. The kiss they'd shared had left him aching and tormented. She sat cross-legged and stretched her hands to the fire, rubbing them together then breathing warm air on them. He wished he could be the one to warm her.

"Andor—" she said.

"If you say thank you for saving your life, I *will* bend you over my knee," he said.

She laughed a little. "Thank you for saving my life."

He groaned and smiled, shaking his head. If he touched her now, he would not be able to resist continuing what they had started, right here, in these icy woods. "You are lucky you have a sword now. Maybe Völundr the smith did help us. We have a horse. We have weapons. We stand a better chance of reaching Jorvik."

Cathy glanced down at the sheathed sword on her waist. "Is it hard? Sword-fighting?"

Andor's stomach growled. He still had the grilled hare legs from yesterday, he just needed to warm them up on the fire and they would do nicely for breakfast. He pierced them with a long stick and put them over the fire.

"Sword-fighting is a skill. Like your yoga. It is hard in the beginning and gets easier with practice. Why?"

She bit her lower lip. "Can you teach me?"

He must have heard her wrong. "Teach you?"

"Yes. You constantly say you will not help me. I don't want to be a burden to you. If you teach me, I can be an asset. You said I have the physique of a warrior."

She was not a burden. He was. She was perfect the way she was, with her strange diet and her desire to help and her kind heart.

If she became a shield-maiden, too—

She would be able to protect herself, which meant she would stand a higher chance of surviving the threats of this world. And maybe—a small part of him whispered somewhere deep inside—he could actually have a future with someone like her.

No, not someone like her. With *her*.

His heart ached so much he choked.

Fool.

"Don't look at me like that," she said. "I want to defend myself."

Andor lowered his eyes to the hare thighs. He had already broken his word to himself by going after her. Even though he had told himself he did not, the truth was that he felt responsible for her life. Even if he taught her to fight, he doubted the feeling of responsibility would be lighter. He doubted he could avoid looking at her and following her every movement to make sure she was safe.

He met her gaze. "I do not think it is a good idea."

"What? Why?"

"Because I am going to protect you. I have already started."

"Yes, Andor. But I also want to protect you."

He laughed. "You? Protect me?"

"Yes. I've already saved your butt, remember?"

"Wielding a sword and dragging an unconscious man into a cave are two different things."

"Yes. But still. I think I can do it. I—" She cut herself off and lowered her gaze, pursing her lips.

"What? What are you not telling me?"

She met his gaze, eyes burning. Andor's stomach turned with the realization that she would not back down.

"I like it," she finished.

"You like holding a sword?"

She stood and unsheathed the weapon. It was made of simple metal, but it fit her size. Cathy looked at it in her hand. Her eyes sparkled, and in them a new strength appeared. She swung the sword a few times—awkwardly and uselessly because she held it wrong, but there was a gracefulness and strength about her movements that made him think that she could be a good warrior.

"Yes," she said, then lowered the tip of the sword to a hare thigh and picked it from the stick, making the stick sway so that Andor barely managed to save the second thigh from falling into the fire. Andor watched open mouthed as she picked the meat from the sword with another hand, bit into it and chewed with a satisfied smile. "I really do."

Then her expression changed to one of surprise and disgust, and she spat the meat into the fire.

"Oh my god, I'm going to be sick," she said. Coals hissed where the pieces of food landed.

Andor shook his head. "Woman, first of all, do not use your sword for eating food. Respect the weapon. Second of all, do not waste a perfectly good breakfast."

He stood and removed the leg from the fire, then bit into it. "It tastes fine."

"Whatever. Will you teach me or not?"

He chewed, studying her. Then he swallowed and sighed. "I cannot say no to a warrior. You have everything—the height, the strength, the spirit. I will teach you. But you must do as you are told."

She squealed like a little girl—so much for being a warrior—and bounced up and down on her toes. "I have one condition," she said.

"*You* have a condition?"

"Yes."

"I am the one teaching. I shall be setting the conditions."

She shook her head slowly and smiled a sly, charming smile that made the corners of his mouth twitch.

"You teach me sword-fighting. And I teach you yoga."

The muscles of his face fell. "No."

"Yes, you know you want to. You know you're curious."

"No!"

"Come on, just once. When else will you have a chance to try something from the future? No one else in this whole part of the world has even heard of yoga."

"If you think this argument will convince me, you are the madwoman I thought you were."

"Just once, Andor. Come on. Please?"

Loki must be stirring his brain like stew right now, because Andor did want to try it. He could not forget the serene expression on Cathy's face. What if he could feel that, too?

"Once," he said.

She squealed again and clapped her hands together.

"Calm down, Cathy, or I will change my mind."

She shook her head. "You'll love it."

He frowned and rolled his eyes, then looked around. "We must find something for you to eat or you'll fall unconscious after the first sword practice."

She beamed at him as though sunlight streamed out of her beautiful eyes. He must be getting mad himself, because he began feeling warmer. For the first moment in a long time the ghosts behind a dark door in his soul kept silent.

CHAPTER FOURTEEN

CATHY GRIMACED as she bit into the tart flesh of a winter crab apple.

"Euch," she mumbled with a shudder. "This is pure acid. Maybe I should reconsider that rabbit leg after all."

By some stroke of luck, they had found a crab apple tree that still held some small red fruit, although birds had been happily feasting on them. Andor had helped Cathy to gather the tiny apples and now they had breakfast.

"Take it." He stretched out the last drumstick.

She eyed it, hunger rising in her stomach. Maybe she *should* start eating meat, just until she got back to her time. It must be healthy during this day and age. Andor was right, scavenging was difficult in the woods in winter, and she was deprived of many important nutrients. She was also exhausted after days of surviving on fewer calories than she needed. She was probably losing weight like crazy, although without protein it was mostly muscle weight not fat, so that didn't do her any favors. Was being vegan the wisest choice during winter a millennium in the past?

She had almost thrown up because she wasn't used to meat anymore, but she had enjoyed delicious meat dishes at home before she'd become a vegan.

"Okay, give it to me," she said. One corner of his mouth crawled up and he passed her the drumstick.

She bit into the aromatic meat, and although it was unusual and a little chewy and strong, it actually complemented the crab apples surprisingly well. And having something warm in her stomach felt divine.

"Mmmmm," she moaned, and closed her eyes briefly.

Her stomach had shrunk so much in the last few days that she was full just from a few crab apples and the leg.

Andor watched her over the fire, his expression thoughtful and soft. "Sleep for a few hours. You are useless on the road being tired like this. When you wake up, we will resume our journey."

Cathy was tired. Her feet were nice and warm in front of the fire, and her limbs ached from struggling with her captors. Now that the danger was behind them and she had eaten something and was warm again, her body was as heavy as a sack of rocks. "Okay, but then you."

"We shall see."

She looked at him, considering something. "Your lap looks very soft," she said.

"What?"

She crawled up next to him instead of answering, stretched out on the ground, and lay her head at the crease of his hip and his leg. She cuddled deeper into her cloak.

"You look tough on the outside, but your lap is strangely cozy," she said, nestling with her head to get comfortable. "See, I'm almost over your knee, just as you wanted."

He didn't move, didn't even breathe, one arm went totally still in the air above her. Then slowly, he lowered it and rested his hand on her shoulder. Even through the layers of clothes, his touch went through her in a wave of sweet warmth. Cathy felt him pull his cloak over her.

She sighed and closed her eyes, his leg firm and warm under her cheek, his stomach moving against the back of her head as he breathed.

As Cathy started to drift off, the memory of Brad's head lying on her lap filled her mind. They'd been dating for a month and it was the first time he'd spent the night, the first time they'd been intimate. She couldn't believe he liked her, and had expected him to leave like a jerk the next morning. But he didn't. He stayed for breakfast. Later, they went out for lunch at a vegan street-food festival. Then they went to the beach and he taught her how to surf, after which they had sat on the sand, and Brad had lain his head in her lap just like she was doing with Andor now.

She had brushed Brad's wet curly hair, like liquid gold against his tanned skin, and gently caressed his face. His eyes had been closed and he'd moaned, smiling.

"I think I'm falling for you, Cathy," he'd said, then froze and looked at her, his blue eyes soft and fragile.

Her chest had exploded in tenderness, and tears had gathered in the corners of her eyes. Her affirmations must have been working because the man of her dreams lay in her lap looking at her like that. Speaking words of love.

"Me, too, Brad," was all she could manage.

And now Brad was so many years away from her. And if he wasn't on life support, he'd be gone.

Gone...

Was she really accepting that?

A tear crawled from her eye down to Andor's trousers. "Was it hard, when she died?" she asked.

He tensed, the muscles of his thigh turning into hardwood under her cheek, his stomach behind her back a flat stone.

"What?"

"I—I might need to accept the possibility that Brad will die. So I want to know how to deal with that. How did you?"

He didn't answer for a long time, and when he did, his voice came out cracked and broken. "I may not be the one you should ask. I do not think that I did."

"Oh."

Cathy watched the fire, acutely aware of Andor's tension. His pain was almost palpable through his hard skin. "Is that what's haunting you? Your wife?"

"No." He shifted. "She is not haunting me. It was my fault. I killed her."

Cathy sat up, her eyes wide. He met her gaze with a grimace of sorrow, his eyes bloodshot and watery, his face ashen.

"What?" she said.

"We were wed not but a year when I went raiding with the Viking forces in Bretland. I had promised her that I would return before the harvest festival. But Ubba asked me to raid the Wilham Monastery and get the jeweled Bible. Ubba knew that the king would pay dearly in fertile farmland, which is why we invaded in the first place. Ubba could have thrown thousands of men into a battle to win those lands, but he had a better idea of how to outwit the Saxons. Using cunning and the enemy's weakness to gain what we seek without losing lives is a good thing. A smart thing. I could have refused Ubba, but he'd promised me to make me his second-in-command. Following my pride, my drive for glory and fame, I broke my word to Svana. I thought that she'd rejoice over the riches I would bring home, the land I would win us. That she'd forgive me my neglect when I showered her with gold and silver."

He swallowed hard then talked through clenched teeth. "But she never harbored any anger towards me. She was busy protecting herself and our people from Jarl Elgr's men who had come for my treasure. I returned as the village was being attacked and burned, and they waited for us. Svana had been stabbed... She died in my arms."

Cathy's eyes filled with tears again.

"If only I had not followed my ambition but come back when I promised. Ubba would have found someone else to raid the monastery. But she would be alive. I killed her. Her and my whole village. Charred beams now stand where people lived for generations. As strong a warrior as I am, I cannot protect those I love."

Cathy's heart squeezed. She scooched closer and took his hand. His skin was rough and calloused, and his fingers were cold. She rubbed them between her palms.

"My fiancé died—*almost* died—because he protected me," she said. "And I'd rather he hadn't. I'm sure she felt the same."

He inhaled sharply, his nostrils flaring, his jaw muscles working under his beard.

"If she loved you, Andor, there is no way she blamed you for any of that. You shouldn't, either."

He glanced up into the milky gray sky lying low above the dark branches of the trees, his face as tense as a mask. A raven crowed somewhere.

Cathy's eye burned with unshed tears. She wondered if Andor's wife was up there somewhere. Or if Brad was. Maybe they both were present in some way. Maybe they were like angels, watching over Andor and her.

Andor returned his gaze to her, his eyes dark with pain. "I would like to believe that. But even if it is true, I can never forgive myself. Not when endangering her life was so clearly in my hands. All I had to do was keep my promise to her and come back home when I was supposed to."

Cathy squeezed his rough hand in hers and put her head on his shoulder.

"Even that weak monk, Aethelred, who cannot lift a sword, has more strength than me. He forgave me. But I do not think I should be forgiven, Cathy."

Helplessness weakened Cathy's shoulders. She couldn't make him forgive himself. He needed to find his own way to do that, and she hoped that he would, with time. All she could do was offer him comfort.

And she hoped that time would work a miracle for her, too, and take her back to the future. Although, strangely, the urge to return to the life she knew shrank daily.

CHAPTER FIFTEEN

"Does that look empty to you?" Cathy said, pointing between two rolling hills.

She sat in front of him on the horse. With her luscious behind between his thighs, today's trip was the most pleasant he had been on in ages. Now dusk was starting to fall, and the horse was getting tired, so they had left the road in search of a place to spend the night.

Andor squinted in the direction Cathy pointed and saw two wooden buildings with thatched roofs.

"It is hard to say." He brought the horse to a halt. "I shall go and check. If someone is inside, it is better that they do not hear us approach. Stay here."

He jumped off the horse and helped her dismount, too. Then he unsheathed his sword and went to the houses. The farm had likely either been abandoned or raided—if someone still lived there, they would almost certainly have a fire burning and candles lit against the coming night. The door to what looked like a cowshed was open and hay was scattered on the dirt floor. The second building had a south-facing window with wooden blinds. The door was open. He stood and listened but heard nothing but the distant burbling of flowing water—probably a stream or a river—the wind and the rustling of the woods that lay three dozen steps away. There was a vegetable garden behind the house, empty.

Andor peered inside the house and allowed his eyes to adjust to the darkness. There were signs of battle—broken clay jars and wooden utensils littered the reed floor. The smell of dust and decay hung in the air. A hearth stood in the middle with a cauldron. Andor's stomach rumbled at the thought of a hot stew, something other than grilled hare.

His eyes fell on the single bed and he closed them briefly. He would sleep on the floor because he would not be able to restrain himself if he slept in the same bed with Cathy. She was already promised to another and was eager to get back to him. Andor should be careful not to allow her into his heart.

The owners would probably not be back. So unless other travelers decided to stay here for the night, they should be safe and would have their first decent rest in a long time.

Andor went back for Cathy, who took the news of their night's lodgings with a heartwarming smile that made him grin, too.

Inside the house, she looked at the hearth and the cauldron with the same hope that boiled within him.

"Are you saying that we might have something warm to eat today?" she asked.

"We might. Go check the garden, maybe there are still some vegetables left in the soil. I shall bring water and firewood."

He gave water to the horse, cut the wood, and came back into the house. Cathy was peeling parsnips, and white carrots lay on the table next to her.

"There is a root cellar over there." She pointed at a small

trapdoor in the floor in the far corner of the house. "I'll cook up some soup or a stew with what I can find in there, and maybe a rabbit would be nice."

Andor put the water on the floor and the wood he had cut in the hearth. "I shall find one then."

He started the fire and put water in the cauldron to start heating. As he went out the door to look for a rabbit, he glanced back at the room and the sight made his chest ache.

It was so homey. The warmth of the fire in the hearth, his woman cooking dinner, him going hunting. Everything he had forbidden himself to have...was afraid to have. And yet, deep down, he wanted it more than his next breath.

Cathy looked up at him, surprised that he was standing in the doorway. Their eyes met for a moment. She was so beautiful he stopped breathing.

But she was not his and never would be.

Before she could ask anything, he turned and walked away.

In the darkening woods, he soon caught two rabbits. He dressed them and took them in for Cathy to put in the stew. The scent in the hut was mouthwatering, and he watched Cathy's face brighten as she threw herbs in the cauldron.

"There was even salt down there," she said. "Very crude salt with a bit of dirt, but still." Her eyes fell on the game. "Oh! Two. Put them in, please."

When he did as she asked, she said. "All right, now all that's left is for us to wait."

Andor looked around. "Please tell me Thor left us a cask of mead in that cellar."

"Mead? The honey beer? Ah right, that's what you guys drink. No, unfortunately, no alcohol. Wouldn't mind a drink, though. But I was thinking, while we wait for food, how about you show me some sword moves?"

Andor chuckled. It was a good way to distract him from the close, warm space, the bed, and her.

"Get your sword," he said and walked out.

Outside, the night had settled around them, and it was dark—which was good, at least, because it was unlikely they would be spotted from the road.

Andor unsheathed his sword and stood holding it with both hands at shoulder level. Memories of Hvaldalen rushed at him: the green hills, giant mountains, dark forests, and the still mirror of the fjord curving around them. He remembered when his father, Jarl Thorn, taught him sword-fighting for the first time. His younger brother, Bari, who had been only five winters old then, watched him with fascination. Bari had not been a healthy child and had died a few moons later because of a winter fever. The memory carved a hollow feeling in Andor's chest—of the brother he had never seen grow up, of the home that had burned because of him and stood now empty, charred, and abandoned.

What would his father have said to him?

He would be ashamed of his son running away. He would be ashamed of the son who had failed to protect his woman and his people.

No. Away. He had to get away from those ghosts. He needed to lose himself in action again.

"Stand like this," he said to Cathy. "Left foot ahead, right foot behind. Hips straight and facing me. Take the sword to your right shoulder, and hold it straight like so. This is a basic movement, a simple strike from above. Bring your sword forward to protect yourself from an unexpected counterattack."

He demonstrated the action and watched Cathy repeat his movements. He gave an approving nod when she did as he said.

"Step a little to your right so that you are out of your enemy's line of attack. Now bring down the blade in a straight line and hit your opponent."

He lowered the sword and touched her gently on her shoulder. She performed the attack.

"Good. You have strong arms and a long reach, and, therefore, an advantage against many people who are short. Now repeat the movement."

Cathy stepped to her right and swung down the sword without bringing her arms forward enough, which he pointed out to her. He made her repeat the movement several times, each time enjoying the gracefulness of her body, which was beautiful to see but would not do her any favors in battle.

"You are too gentle," he said. "This is not yoga."

"Well—"

"No. You must not be afraid to hurt your enemy. This is about life and death."

The thought of someone much stronger and more skilled than her coming at her made his skin chill.

"Repeat, with more strength, more anger."

She did, over and over, and he watched her, corrected her. But she continued making the same mistake.

He moved to stand behind her, placing his hands on her hips, and almost drew his hands back from the jolt that ran through him like a wave of heat. Her hips were both firm and soft and nicely rounded. She tensed under his palms and stopped breathing.

He licked his suddenly dry lips and pressed into her hips slightly to guide them to a straight position. "Like so," he said. He should remove his hands. Now. "Now bring the sword forward."

She did. She should tell him to take his hands off her.

"Step forward with your right leg."

Her muscles moved under his palms as she shifted her weight, and he wanted to trace the shape of her body.

No. *Remove your hands, you oaf.*

He moved with her.

"Bring the sword down," he said.

She brought the sword down, dropped it to the grass, whirling to face him in a flash of golden hair and gray eyes, and her lips were on his.

She kissed him with softness and with heat, waking a whole whirlwind of fire in him, and he did not have the strength to stop. He picked her up, threw her over his shoulder like plunder, enjoying the feel of her gorgeous arse under his palm, and carried her into the house.

Maybe a forever with her was not in his destiny, but she wanted him now. And just for now, just for tonight, he could imagine that she was his, he was hers, and this was home.

CHAPTER SIXTEEN

Andor threw Cathy onto the bed, and the straw mattress was hard as she landed on her back, but she didn't care. It got her even more turned on. He came at her as though there was no other option, as though she drew him with a force. Their eyes were locked, connected in a closed space where there was no one and nothing but them.

Andor stood at the edge of the bed, broad shouldered and narrow hipped, a bearded warrior with a familiar face and an unfamiliar soul. The aromas of woodsmoke and cooking stew mingled with the scent of Andor—all leather and iron and man—and Cathy dissolved in it, taking it all in, her body expanding beyond its borders.

She spread her arms to the sides, her fingers tracing the rough, prickly surface of the mattress, her body melting under Andor's burning eyes as he followed her every move.

"Take off your clothes," he said.

He sounded so possessive and bossy—and a surge of bliss spread through her. With shaking hands, she undid the belt of her tunic, her skin sensitive against the linen. She had to rid herself of it, needing Andor's hands on her.

Then she took the edges of the tunic and drew it up and over her head, still wearing her spandex vest.

"That is one beautiful garment, but not as beautiful as you are. Off."

Cathy bit her lip. The moment when Andor had seen her in the stream had nothing on this. If she thought he had wanted her then, now his eyes consumed her. She gripped the edges of the top and dragged it over her head. Warm air tingled her naked breasts, her nipples tightening into stiff peaks under Andor's eyes. She tensed. He'd see her naked. Not from a distance like before, but up close. Every stretch mark, every ounce of fat, every fold. She closed her eyes, embarrassed and yet still aroused.

"Open your eyes," he said. "See me."

Cathy swallowed, gathered her strength and opened her eyes.

"Good," he said and slowly undid his belt. Then off came his tunic, and a glorious feast of a Grade A man appeared before her.

Cathy's mouth went dry at the sight. His shoulders were broad, bulging with muscles. His big and powerful pecs like flat hills. He had a narrow waist with a ripped stomach that tapered into a chiseled V of muscles above his low-hanging trousers. His arms were like tree trunks. His skin was covered with scars—some silver, some pink, and some fresh and red. A tattoo of a dragon breathing fire made in ornate Viking patterns covered his right side.

She wanted that glorious body to cover her, to glide against her, to wrap around her.

How could he be so perfect when she was a collection of unfortunate contradictions?

Andor lowered himself to the bed and stretched alongside her, his masculine scent making her mouth water. As his eyes crawled down her body, her skin burned everywhere his sizzling gaze touched. She arched her back, pushing her breasts out instinctively to make her waist thinner, just like every time she was naked in front of a man.

But he said, "You are too thin. No matter, you are beautiful in any form or shape."

Her world shifted, and her head spun.

"These curves..." he murmured, tracing his rough finger down her breast, her stomach. She sucked it in, not because she wanted to appear smaller but because his touch spread waves of pleasure through her. His hand reached the edge of her trousers.

"Off," he said, his voice deep and husky.

Cathy stared at him. Was she bold enough to remove the rest of her clothes in front of him? Her breath rushed in and out.

"I want you to take them off," he said.

Cathy licked her hot, swollen lips and did as he asked. She was left in only her swimming shorts.

He looked at them with a smirk, then hooked the edge with his index finger. "I wondered what these were. No matter. They do not belong on you. Allow me."

He loomed over her, still on the bed, a mountain shielding the light of the fire behind him. He took the edges of her shorts and pulled them down. The spandex slid down easily. Oh god, she wasn't even waxed or shaved. Heat rose in her cheeks and spread across her chest as more of her body was exposed to this gorgeous man who took her breath away with or without clothes.

"You look mouthwatering no matter if you wear clothing or do not," he murmured against her ankle, then kissed it and made his way up, sending small, soft bursts of sweet agony through her skin with every kiss. Or maybe it was from his words. He reached her hip and followed the curve with his lips, continuing up the sensitive skin of her stomach. She arched her body into his mouth, her hands clenching the straw pillow behind her head.

"Can't believe you are saying that," she whispered.

He moved to her breasts and cupped one, then took it into his mouth and began massaging and sucking and licking at the same time. A whirlwind of hot sparks spread through her.

"What?" he asked.

"I—Oh...I can't believe you find me attractive."

He stilled, then straightened his arms and loomed over her. His face was dark, shadowed by the fire behind him. "What did you say?"

Cathy couldn't close her mouth. She physically tried, but it wouldn't close. Had she really just said that out loud? She barely even admitted she thought those things to herself...

"Nothing."

"You do not believe I find you attractive?" his voice rumbled, low and threatening.

Cathy swallowed. *Idiot! That is so not the thing to say to a man. Never reveal your body insecurities to them.*

"I—"

She sat up and tried to cover herself, but Andor held her arms. Cathy couldn't believe she'd started that discussion in the middle of what was the hottest, sexiest experience of her entire life. "I'm fat, okay. I'm afraid you won't find me attractive. You, a gorgeous man, all confidence and glory." She exhaled sharply to relieve the knot in her stomach. "There's the door. Feel free to leave an Andor-shaped hole in it."

"*Fat?*" he repeated, shaking his head. "You are the most beautiful woman that I have ever met. Feminine yet strong. All curves and muscles. A woman and a warrior. A Valkyrie. Not a tiny mouse I can crush with my weight. You have the most delicious body I have ever seen. I have dreams of you riding me. I do not think there was ever a more perfect woman that walked in Midgard."

Her eyes prickled, and one tear crawled down her cheek.

"Certainly not where I come from," she said.

He scooped her into his arms and sat her on his lap. Then kissed the tear away. "I do not know the Los Angeles world. But let me show you how perfect you are in my world."

He kissed her, spreading the wet saltiness between their lips. His kiss was both possessive and gentle. It was deep but soft, and soon she was melting again in his arms. She wanted to believe him. The strokes of his calloused palms, the swipes of his tongue against hers, sent bliss through every cell of her body.

She wanted him, wanted to learn everything about his body and bring him pleasure. Andor moved his mouth to her cheek and began kissing her jaw, then nibbled down her neck, spurring her desire. When he reached her breasts and took one in his mouth, licking, stroking, sucking, all thoughts evaporated from her head. All she could hear were her moans and whimpers as hot honey spread through her veins from his touches.

Continuing to pleasure her breasts with his mouth, Andor slid his hand down her stomach towards her sex. Cathy tensed a little, and the negative voice began blabbering in her head. Andor stopped for a moment. "No," he said. "You are tensing. Whatever happens in your head, stop it. Be with me. Savor this moment."

Cathy breathed out the tension, and his hand continued down into the hair at the apex of her thighs. And a different, sweet kind of tension began burning there. His finger dipped into her folds, and he began exploring, gently and slowly.

"Ahhhh," she moaned, sinking into waves of liquid sunshine.

She arched into his mouth, her head falling back as she closed her eyes. His finger found the sweetest spot in her body, and she jerked a little, tensing and arching even more. He groaned a little in approval and circled her clitoris, spinning the whirlpool of exquisite agony in her body faster and faster. Perspiration burst through Cathy's skin, her arousal soaking her entrance, and she moved her hips in time with his seductive rhythm. She ran her palms over his body, his smooth skin, the hills of his muscles, the crisp hair on his chest. He began moaning, too, and his movements became faster, more urgent.

The hot buildup in Cathy reached its peak, and she groaned. "Andor, if you don't stop now—"

"Do, sweet. I want you to."

Oh, mother of pearl... Her core tensed, and built, and built, and finally she couldn't stop it if she tried—she exploded in waves of delicious fire, dissolving, evaporating. For a breath, she stopped existing.

A moment later, when she came back to awareness, shaking a little with the aftershocks of her orgasm, she found herself in Andor's arms. He wore a satisfied grin.

But she wanted more. She wanted him.

She needed him.

Something had shifted today—in her, in him, in the world.

She pushed him slightly so that he fell onto his back on the mattress. He let out a surprised chuckle.

"You wanted me to ride you," she said and watched his brows crawl up. "Your dreams are about to come true."

She had no idea where it came from, this confidence, this

oneness with herself—her body and soul—and with him. But she'd take it.

The smile fell from his face, his eyes dark and full of desire. Her core, still sensitive and swollen, clenched in delicious anticipation.

Cathy undid his trousers and pushed them down his hips. His thick, hard erection made her clench even more. "Oh," she said and swallowed. "Wow."

When he lay naked in front of her, all muscles and strength, he put one arm behind his head. His erection twitched and Cathy's inner muscles clenched in return. She wanted him inside her, stretching her, filling her, making her his. Making him hers.

Hers.

Slowly, Cathy ran her palms against his long, muscular legs, and Andor's chest began rising and falling slower and deeper.

"You do not look so bad yourself, mister," she said, her voice coming out husky and low.

He twitched his lips slightly within his beard, his eyes going even darker. "What will you do to show this to me?"

Cathy was right in front of his erection now and licked her lips. She took it in both her hands, and it jerked, long and thick and hard, and she became even wetter. She stroked it up and down gently several times, then leaned down and licked his hot, velvety skin, once, twice, three times. Andor closed his eyes, the sinews of his neck bulged, his jaw muscles tensed.

Cathy put her leg over him, placed him against her entrance and plunged down on him. She was swollen and tight, and she gasped as her sensitized flesh filled with overwhelming pleasure. He thrust so deep it hurt slightly and stretched her even more, making her clench around him. Andor moaned, and Cathy felt him twitch within her.

She began moving, savoring the universe of sensations he gave her. She rode him slowly, up and down, feeling him gliding within her, pleasing her, consuming her. He watched her at first, from under half-closed eyelids, but then began thrusting, matching her rhythm. He stretched his hands out and cupped her breasts, massaging them, teasing her nipples. He traced the curve of her waist, and as his hands moved to her hips he grabbed hold. He groaned and began grinding into her with a wildness.

It undid the last of her negative thoughts, the last of any doubt or restrictions, and she gave in fully. And with it, a buildup the likes of which she never had experienced began within her. She was one with him, in this sacral dance, allowing every sensation to flow through her.

Sensation upon sensation bombarded her, the tension unbearable. Then it burst and opened up into a world of sun and warmth and rapture.

Somewhere she wasn't alone.

And as her body took over, so did his, and they rocked together on the surf of a sweet storm for what felt like an eternity.

Cathy collapsed on top of Andor, breathing with him, soaking wet. A tear crawled down her cheek and landed on his chest in a tiny drop. As she watched it, Cathy knew that Andor would be a part of her as long as she lived.

And then she remembered another man who would be part of her forever, a man who was lying in a hospital bed, his life depending on her.

A man she was, apparently, already forgetting.

CHAPTER SEVENTEEN

January 20, 878 AD

"How do you touch your toes like that?" Andor crouched over his feet, doubled up. No matter how much he sweated, no matter how deeply he breathed through the pain, he was failing to straighten his legs and reach his toes at the same time.

While he was going through Helheim, Ragnarok, and what felt like the fire breath of the dragon Fafnir, Cathy glided through the air with flexibility and grace. Her torso pressed against her straight legs, she hugged her knees and buried her face between them. Which gave him the most beautiful view of the backs of her long legs and her behind, which stuck out in the air.

A small mercy, at least.

He already missed that arse, even though he had spent the whole of last night enjoying its sweet company. He had loved Cathy's silky skin against his, her moans as he brought her to ever higher levels of pleasure. They had eaten the stew, sitting on the bed still naked, throwing playful smiles at each other, and then he had fallen asleep holding her in his arms just before dawn. It was quiet in his head—the ghosts were silent for once—and he was happy for the first time since Svana's death.

He was ready for more nights like that. A lifetime of them.

The thought chilled his body. This was not how he was supposed to feel towards Cathy. Towards anyone.

He must have been staring because her face appeared from behind her leg and she exclaimed with indignation, "Andor, get back to padahastasana. And breathe!"

He growled and looked at his toes.

"Now, a big step with your left foot." Cathy made the movement, and Andor followed. "Bend the right knee to make a sharp angle. Stretch the left leg back. Heel back, as though your whole left leg is a straight line. Feel the burn? Good. Arms straight up, as though reaching for the sky. Arch the spine and tilt your head slightly back, but look straight. It's called the equestrian pose, see? Now breathe through your third eye like I taught you."

Andor followed her instructions, and this pose was more pleasant than the previous one. Equestrian pose required both the strength of his legs and stretching. His thigh still pained him, but he was glad to do this and not to lie around like a helpless log. Stretching was the most difficult for him. He found the positions when he needed to support his body with the strength of his muscles child's play because he was used to rowing a boat for hours, which required much strength and endurance. Stretching his stiff sinews, on the other hand, brought to life parts of his body he had no idea existed.

What he liked the most, though, was that the magic of yoga he had observed before as a flow, as one story, was separated into distinctive positions, like building a three-row shieldwall.

And then there was the third eye.

During yesterday's long horse ride, Cathy had started to explain it to him. Apparently, it was situated just above the space between his eyebrows. She had even made him try to breathe through it. He imagined he had a big eyeball between his eyebrows, staring into the distance. But the image did not bring him any peace. And how was it possible to breathe through an eyeball?

"This is useless," he had said. "I feel like a fool."

"Don't give up. It's unlikely it will work right away. You'll see once we do the exercises," she had assured him.

And today, just now, something had happened within him. Again, he imagined he had a third eye—but it was not an eyeball anymore. It was like a single point of concentrated sunlight. As he breathed, a new strength came rushing through his body. He could stretch further, he could bend lower, he could breathe easier.

But it was not just physical strength.

Somehow, the glimpses of peace he had felt when he had watched Cathy do yoga for the first time, touched him and stayed within him. And in that peace, there was no past, no future, and no guilt.

There was only here and now, and he had a glimpse of the life that could be his if he forgave himself.

But he could not.

With a jerk, he opened his eyes. Guilt gutted him. He had sworn never to betray Svana's memory. And yet what was he doing? Was he not betraying her? Allowing himself happiness he did not deserve?

Andor withdrew from the position and stood up, his nostrils flaring. Yoga was a bad idea. Yoga was not distracting him from the ghosts. It was forcing him to face them.

He could not.

The scent of wet woodsmoke, the sight of Svana dying in his arms among the charred skeletons of his people's homes, the last words she'd whispered to him in her gentle voice, "I wanted to be a good wife to you..."

All he could do was run.

"Now put your palms on the ground on both sides of your foot," Cathy said, oblivious that behind her, Andor had already stopped.

He walked past her into the farmhouse.

"We should go," he threw back as he passed her.

"Wait, we're not finished! Andor!"

"I am. It was a mistake. No more yoga. Get your things. When we stop for food, we will double your sword-fighting training. I have no intention of saving your arse next time someone decides to attack us."

He did not look back, but he knew that if he did, he would see that he had hurt her.

And even though it made him feel even worse, he needed to remember to keep his distance. The closeness he felt with her, the things he had confided in her, were an illusion. Like a drunken feast when one had too much mead, forgot about anything else, and had to suffer the consequences the next day.

It was the next day now. And he was sober.

CHAPTER EIGHTEEN

January **25, 878 AD**

"Right. Left. Duck. Right. Left," Andor shouted each time he struck his sword against Cathy's.

The grass they were training on was frosted, but it had melted where the morning sun already touched it. The rhythmical ring of metal against metal disturbed the peaceful gurgling of the stream behind him.

It had been their morning ritual for the past five days on the road. Before they continued their journey, he would train her until he thought her muscles had learned the new movements. When they stopped for a midday meal and to let the horse rest, he would resume teaching her.

Before sword-fighting, he would watch her do her yoga routine, and wish he could join her. But he would walk away because even watching her brought a sense of peace and connection with himself, which made him turn towards the ghosts he so desperately avoided.

Now, he could not walk away, and he could not stop making love to her every night. Sleeping outside during winter, they needed to keep warm, and the best way to do that was lying together. Which he happily did. Daily, he promised himself he would no longer indulge. He was stepping into dangerous territory, caring about her too much. If something happened and he failed to save her, he would not be able to live with himself.

But his body did not care. As soon as her beautiful arse was pressed against him, as soon as the scent of her hair touched his nostrils, his body reacted, and the need to be with her, to plunge into her depths rang louder than the screams of his soul.

And he gave in.

Every night he had her, and she took him willingly.

And now…

Maybe his strikes rang too loud. Maybe he landed his blows too strongly.

But she could take it.

Her arms were strong, and she had learned the movements quickly. Maybe it was all the body work that she was used to doing daily, but Andor was surprised to find that there really was a shield-maiden or a Valkyrie in this woman.

"Ouch!" she screamed as the tip of his sword pierced her shoulder.

He clenched his jaws, resisting the urge to come to her aid. If she was a warrior from his band, or anyone else, he would just laugh it off with them. But now he hated himself for causing her the slightest amount of pain. He needed to stop these feelings.

"Injuries are expected during training."

She massaged her shoulder. "Still, I barely deflected you."

Andor spun around and looked at the road which lay fifty

feet or so away. "You wanted to train. This is training. We have been lucky these past days, but that luck may end after the next turn of the road. We are nowhere near Jorvik."

She crossed her arms over her chest. "Well, do you think I've made progress, at least? You've never said if you think I'm doing all right. You either scold me or keep quiet."

He looked at her big, pretty, hopeful eyes, a shadow of pain in their depths. She was very good. But saying so would make it worse between them. If he wanted to keep his distance, he needed to keep that to himself.

"The enemies will be the judges of that, not me." He shifted his weight from foot to foot, uneasy with where this conversation might be leading them. "Let us be on our way. That is enough for today."

"Wait. You've been so distant lately, ever since that night. I thought...there was something between us, but is it only sex? I can't seem to help my body's response. But I feel like I'm betraying Brad. Every time we sleep together, I feel more ashamed. Especially when you're so cold to me afterwards."

This was exactly what he was trying to avoid.

Run.

"No, Cathy. I will not talk about this."

"Why?"

He turned around and walked to their makeshift camp.

"Because it would be *talking* about this."

He began saddling the horse. He heard Cathy approach behind him.

"But I do want to talk about it. If you feel as guilty as I do—"

He turned to her, his heart raging in his chest. "I said no."

"But we keep having sex and then you're like this. I want to know why. Did I do something?"

"Ask me one more question and you can forget about the sword-fighting lessons."

She pursed her lips and lifted her chin. He hated to see her like that—confused, angry, her shoulders tense instead of holding her head high—and he was the reason for her pain.

But he had no choice. He should have never initiated anything with her, but oh Freyja and Frigg, that had been impossible. Cathy had brought him the joy and comfort his soul had craved. And once he had tasted it, he had wanted more. And he did not deserve more.

They gathered the last of their things, and once the horse was saddled they mounted it, Cathy in the back, hugging him, her warm body pressed against his.

The day was sunny and cold, and as the woods and the hills passed by, Andor felt Cathy's tension behind him, and the silence between them was heavier than ever before. When they stopped for rest right after midday, he could have cut the tension with an ax. Cathy clearly had much to say, and she fumed, keeping her anger behind sealed lips.

They ate in silence, and Andor watched as she rubbed her palms in front of the fire. He wished he could cover them and warm them with his breath.

"Let us train and be on our way." He rose to his feet and picked up his sword.

Cathy rose, too, and stood in the position he had taught her. "Let me make a deal with you."

"A deal?"

"Yes. I'm tired of your silent ass running away. I know you feel guilty. I do, too. I feel like I'm letting Brad down. And I think you feel something similar, but you refuse to face those feelings."

He gripped his sword tighter. Her words echoed against the

door that shut out the ghosts, and they began clawing to be set free.

"What is the deal?" he said through gritted teeth.

"You fight me. Do not hold back. If you win, we continue in your cowardly, running away manner. If I win—you know, scratch you or unarm you—we sit and talk. No holding back."

"Do you fully understand what you just did?"

"I believe I challenged you."

Inside, fury filled him with something that resembled the roar of fire. "You called me a coward."

She straightened her shoulders and lifted her chin.

"And I stand by my words. You may physically be the strongest man I've ever met. But inside, you refuse to face whatever is haunting you. Bring it on, Andor. I look forward to kicking your silent ass."

Run!

He could not possibly harm a woman. Not the woman who—

Who what? He had vowed to protect?

Wrong.

Who could not protect herself?

Probably wrong.

Who he felt responsible for?

Andor's mouth tightened.

Right.

He clenched his fists.

Honesty always came with a price. He should not feel responsible. He had been clear with Cathy from the beginning.

And yet, why was he feeling everything he had forbidden himself to feel?

Fool. What a fool. And she—a truth-searching, soul-seeking, loins-heating vixen. She should be stopped. She'd never win the deal anyway.

"I will show you," Andor said. "Do not dare to manipulate me like that. Be ready. Protect yourself."

He launched at her and she parried, his sword sliding away from her. He came again and again, metal ringing against metal, but she deflected him every time with surprising strength. She attacked him, and he staggered back. She would have unarmed him if he had not held his sword with enough strength.

"Arghh!" she yelled as she came at him now with full force, her face distorted with battle fury.

A Valkyrie.

She could take him. The ghosts banged and shouted against the door.

If only you kept your promise, we would be alive. You might have a son by now. You could hold your wife in your arms. Your father would never have allowed this to happen. He always put his people before his own selfishness.

No.

Silence!

Andor could not allow her to win. If he talked to her, the ghosts would be out in the open.

Fear, guilt, shame came howling—to protect him, to haunt him, to keep him down.

He roared and attacked from the side.

When his blade met the resistance of her flesh, he stopped and withdrew right away. He was not fighting an enemy. He was fighting the woman he—

Loved.

She screamed and fell to her knees.

Andor tossed aside his sword and rushed to her, fighting her arms away to look at what he had done to her.

"Get away!" she yelled. "Get your hands off me."

He knelt by her side, watching helplessly as she pulled

away her cloak and lifted her tunic to look at her side. There was a shallow slash against the lower, softer side of her waist. The wound was clean and not deep.

"That does not need to be sutured," Andor said, his hands itching to bandage it. The wound was bleeding, but it was not a threat to her life...unless she got a rot-wound. Still, guilt weighed on him and tore his chest apart. "Let me bandage it, at least."

"No, stay away from me," she said, furious. "Let me bandage it, at least," she mocked.

She pushed down the tunic and belted it.

"Congratulations." She stood and picked up her sword. "You won. Rejoice in being a cowardly jerk, running away from the life you could have. We will remain silent until we reach York and then part ways forever. I shouldn't have involved myself with you anyway. I can't believe I betrayed Brad with *you*. Forgot about him because of *you* while he is lying in a hospital bed, about to wake up at any moment. He deserves better than this. I'll go clean this. Do not dare follow me."

With that, she snatched up her hat, which had fallen off during their fight, and walked into the woods.

Andor watched her leave. Should he go after her? Talk about it?

No. He had just silenced the ghosts. Even they could not stand seeing him harm her like that.

His feet were frozen to the ground, and his heart beat against his ear drums. And for the first time in his life, Andor felt like a coward.

CHAPTER NINETEEN

THE SUN WAS SETTING when Cathy started to make her way back to the camp.

She couldn't stand being near Andor until she'd had time to calm down. She had cleaned the wound with icy cold water from the stream and done yoga and meditation despite her side aching. Andor had actually hurt her. If his blade had cut any deeper, she would have been in serious trouble. She'd thought they'd only train, not try to kill each other.

Why had he done that? Did he want to make a point that he couldn't give a shit about her and that he could even harm her?

She was such an idiot. She didn't know anyone stupider than she was. All he wanted was an easy lay. Maybe he did think she was beautiful. Maybe he had a thing for tall, big-boned girls.

Whatever the reason, it was clear he felt nothing for her. That he didn't feel the way she felt.

And how did she feel?

Confused. Betrayed. Guilty.

In love.

What an idiot. She was falling for the guy. He showed her a drop of emotional connection, and she was all over him. Typical. When all she should be thinking about was getting back to Brad and saving his life.

Brad. Gorgeous, smart, kind Brad. What would she do without him? Without him, there would be no one left who'd accept her for who she was. Not even her family—who loved her, no doubt, but who were numero uno to judge her.

"Are you sure you want to eat that?" her mother would ask if Cathy had a vegan cookie in her hand.

"You ate *meat*?" her sister would say if she knew Cathy had eaten grilled hare, and she'd probably put up an Instagram story about that for her one million subscribers to see and judge.

"Sweetheart, take my gym membership. The yoga is clearly not enough," Dad would say.

She could even see how her own students, who loved her lessons, wondered how a vegan yoga instructor still had all those layers of fat.

Here it didn't matter if she looked five or ten pounds lighter or heavier. Here all that mattered was that you were healthy and strong enough to survive. In fact, Andor seemed to appreciate her strength and height. And she had begun to feel grateful for her healthy body.

She had always known there were more important things in life than how you looked, but since she'd arrived in the Viking Age, she had truly started to believe it in her soul.

The camp was just ahead of her now, but even before she reached it, she could hear many male voices. She gripped the handle of her sword, afraid to move an inch, her breath coming out shakily. She couldn't make out exactly what they were saying, but she could tell they were speaking Old English.

Her hands shaking, she slowly moved forward. She needed to know what was going on. Was Andor among them?

God, was Andor even alive?

She crept quietly between the trees and hid behind one of them, close enough that she could hear what they were saying but they couldn't see her.

She glanced from behind the trunk. There were dozens of them, maybe thirty or forty. There were horses, and the men were all heavily armed and wearing chain mail and helms.

Then she saw him. By the campfire, Andor kneeled, and a richly dressed man held a sword to his neck. Cathy's hands and feet chilled. Andor looked at the Saxon with such silent hatred that if his eyes could kill, the man would have long been dead.

"Although you are dressed like a Saxon, I do not believe you are," the man said. "Not after I have found this." He had something in his hand, and when he raised it and shook the piece of cloth, Cathy saw that it was the quarter-circle of the raven banner. The man waited for Andor's reaction, and when his only response was a scowl, he continued. "You do not wish to speak, Dane? Let me tell you, I have means to make you. One last time, where are your companions? Huh? Guthrum, where is he?"

She knew she had no chance against so many armed men. Attacking them would be suicide. She should go. She could make her way up to York, pretend she was a boy. If she met someone on the way, they wouldn't think she was a woman. Not with a sword. She knew how to survive here now: start a fire, catch some sort of wildlife, stay off the road. She had a chance without Andor.

She should take it. Every moment she lost here, Brad drew closer to death.

And—god—if she died here, his life would be over, too.

The wisest thing to do was to leave. Abandon Andor. God

knew he deserved being left, after he'd wounded her. After he'd withdrawn. After he'd—

Used her.

"Let us be on our way, people," the rich man said, placing his sword in its sheath. "Tie his hands in front of him. He can walk the rest of the way. I want to be back home before nightfall."

As they hustled about, Andor watched them in helpless fury, then looked around the forest. She thought that for one moment his eyes fell on her.

They were so familiar. They were Brad's eyes, but not sunny and full of life and laughter. They were haunted with a pain she wanted to soothe.

She could not leave him. Not in this world, not in another world, not until her heart stopped beating. Even if he did not respond to her feelings. Even if he hated her.

She could not live with herself if she left him now.

Could she ever leave him?

CHAPTER TWENTY

"Let them in! It is Ealdorman Aethelwulf!" someone cried up to the watchtower over the entrance gate of the stronghold.

Cathy had followed the Saxons for a couple of hours. Hidden in the woods, she watched the wooden palisade walls illuminated by the torches in the darkness. The air was thick with the scent of damp wood in the drizzling rain. Andor's captors stood before the gates waiting while the sounds of more cries and fuss came from inside the fortress.

They were saying something, but she could barely hear from here. Crawling a bit closer, she heard, "Execute him in the morning and take his head to Guthrum, that will show him."

Her heart stopped, her hands shaking.

The gates opened and the procession walked through the gates. Andor still looked proud, though he stumbled a little as the horse he was tied to moved forward and the rope around his wrists grew taut. With increasing worry in her gut, Cathy watched as the gates closed behind them with a thump. Should she have tried to blend in with the men to sneak in? No, likely they'd recognize her as an outsider right away and imprison her with Andor.

The fortress was the size of a small stadium. Many soldiers guarded it, so she needed to be smart. If she had anything to trade for Andor's freedom, she would. But all she had besides her clothes was the sword, and she needed it to save him.

After what must have been an hour of watching the fortress, wracking her brain for ideas and discarding them, she heard hooves thumping somewhere behind her and looked down the road. A horse pulled a cart full of brushwood, an old man in a brown monk's robe steering it.

He might be the last person to get inside the fortress tonight, her last chance to save Andor. How ironic that she needed the help of yet another monk when she'd never gone to church a day in her life. She did believe there was a higher power watching over her, though, and she sent out a silent thank-you to the universe.

Quietly, she ran between the trees until she reached the slow-moving cart, staying low as she walked behind it. Glancing inside, she saw there was some space for her and enough twigs and brushwood to cover herself.

She grabbed hold of the back wall and used her increased arm strength to haul herself over as soundlessly as possible, thankful it wasn't too high. The old man turned his head to the side, and Cathy lay flat on the bottom of the cart. When he turned back, she crawled to the heap of brushwood and buried herself in it, pulling the twigs and branches over herself as quietly as she could. She twitched every time a twig snapped, but the hooves of the donkey seemed to muffle the noise she was making. The sharp ends of broken branches dug into the unprotected skin of her face and hands, and one poked the wound on her side, but she gritted her teeth and kept silent.

Soon, she heard a distant "Who is there?"

"'Tis me, ol' Brother Baldwin. The villagers sent you brushwood."

"Let him in."

The gates screeched as they opened, and the cart moved forward again.

"Hope you are comfortable there, lad," the old man said quietly, and Cathy's blood chilled. "Now tell me why you are here. Cause if 'tis ill will, I shall alert the guards so loud, they shall capture you before your heart's next beat. Though, since you have not yet killed me, I do not believe you mean me harm."

Cathy swallowed. "I'm here to free a prisoner."

"What prisoner?"

"A Norseman. They just brought him in. I do not want to kill anyone, but the man is important— He saved me, and I owe him my life. All I want is to free him before they execute him."

The man stopped the cart, and Cathy heard him climb down. Through the branches, she saw his wrinkled face. He began unloading the brushwood.

"Norsemen are the enemies. Why should I help you? They've killed enough God-fearing Christians."

Cathy cursed inwardly. "If they kill him, there will be even more deaths. They intend to take his head to the Viking leader, Guthrum, and threaten him. But it will only make the Vikings more violent."

"How do I know he is Viking and not an outlaw?"

"Here." She removed Andor's silver Thor's hammer from around her neck, wondering why he'd never asked for it back. "This is Viking."

She gave the necklace to him and watched through the gap in the planks of the cart as his eyes widened and he nodded solemnly.

"Wait here," he said.

"Please, promise me you won't report me to the guards."

He kept silent for a moment, and she was afraid that was exactly what he was going to do.

"I promise, lad. I just want to make sure you are telling the truth. If so, I will help you. God knows, I do not want any more bloodshed among good people."

He walked away and Cathy swallowed, her heart beating so loud she couldn't hear anything else. The smell of a feast reached her—they were likely celebrating their success in capturing one of the enemy. It was quiet, only distant voices and laughter.

Then Baldwin returned. "You speak the truth," he said. "The guards told me about a Viking prisoner and the planned execution. I shall help you. You may get out."

She looked around. "No one's watching?"

"No."

She carefully crawled out from under the brushwood, and when she was sure no one was watching, she slid out of the cart. She was next to a building on the left side of a large court-yard, hard-packed earth beneath her feet. Huts stood all around the yard. At some distance, the walls of the palisade loomed with several watchtowers along the perimeter. The gates were twenty or so feet away. To Cathy's right stood what looked like a wooden castle, two stories high, with big carved doors and small, dimly lit windows. A tiny wooden church with a cross above the door stood next to the main house— that must be what the strange castle-like building was— across the courtyard opposite the entrance gates to Cathy's right.

"Where can he be?" she asked.

"Must be in one of the sheds. 'Tis where they hold pris-oners before execution."

Cathy swallowed. "I can't break him free alone."

"I am a man of god and will not take up arms against my own people."

"We must use cunning then. Can you drive us out, the same way I got in?"

He frowned. "No, that will not work. I always unload the brushwood and the following day drive to the villages and bring whatever they give to the ealdorman."

"Well, we have to figure something out."

He sniffed the air and glanced at a hut standing next to the main house. "It smells like ol' Elflede is cooking stew. I shall see if she has any waste left."

Cathy raised her brows. "What?"

"I hope your friend is not squeamish. It might be the only thing they'll let me drive out of the stronghold tonight."

Cathy sighed. "Let's pray this works, Brother Baldwin." She took his dry, calloused hands in hers and looked him straight in the eyes. "Thank you. You might be risking your life to help the enemy."

He nodded softly. "God bless you, child. If it is His will, we will survive this night and spare a violent death to many."

He removed his hands and began unloading the cart. Cathy glanced at the shed he had indicated. People—servants probably—moved around the courtyard, carrying things, and her best bet would be to pretend to be a servant, too. She grabbed an armful of brushwood and walked towards the shed. Two guards stood, one on either side of the door, both of them wearing leather armor and carrying swords. Cathy passed by them as though carrying the brushwood somewhere, and they followed her with their eyes.

She turned around the corner of the next building and put the brushwood on the ground. Her heart thumping in her chest, she let some time pass, as though she was busy doing something, then appeared again and stopped in front of the guards.

She glanced at the tallest and strongest one and said, "You. Ealdorman Aethelwulf wants to see you."

He frowned. "Why?"

"Something about how well you fought. He wants to reward you. He's about to dine and he wants you to dine with him."

"Lucky bastard," the other one muttered.

The man's face brightened a little, and he shifted to walk away. Then he stopped and narrowed his eyes at Cathy. "Who are you?"

"Me?" Sweat broke through Cathy's skin. She licked her lips and coughed, trying to make her voice steady. "Cathan, I'm new. Just came to serve here from the village."

"Ah. Good luck." He shoved the other man in the shoulder. "Have a good night," he said and walked away.

The other one scowled, turning his head, eyes following his friend.

Now or never. Her feet frozen, her hands shaking, she stepped forward and hit the man in the back of the head with the pommel of her sword.

He turned, swaying on his feet. Not hard enough, she thought. His hands went to his sword and tried to get it out, but he was weak. Cathy hit him in the temple, and he fell to the ground like a sack of potatoes. She took his sword and looked at the door. It had a big, heavy lock on it, and she sank to her knees to search the guard for the key. It wasn't there. She stepped back and glanced around, panicked.

She needed to act fast. Shadows passed behind the building. Anyone could come here at any moment.

Moving to the shed, she leaned towards the door. "Andor!" she whispered loudly. "Andor! Are you there?"

Nothing came. Oh no, they couldn't have executed him already, could they?

"Andor!" she cried louder than she wanted.

She heard some shuffling, then a surprised "Cathy?"

Relief flooded her, and she released the air from her lungs in a shaky breath.

"I came to free you, but I don't know where the key is. Are you all right?"

"Go away." His voice sounded weak, and her stomach sank. "Go to Jorvik. They will kill you if they catch you."

"I'm not leaving without you. I even got us a getaway wagon. Just need the key."

"Hey!" someone said, and she spun around to see the tall guard who had walked away. "What the f—"

She launched at him before she could allow herself to get scared and run away. He only just managed to unsheathe his sword in time to deflect her attack. One part of her terrified, her training took over and she kept her cool. Even though it was a cheap move, she kicked him in the balls, and he doubled up with a pained yelp and fell to the ground. With a now-familiar movement, she hit him in the temple. She didn't want to kill people any more than Brother Baldwin did, if she could help it.

He fell next to the other man. Breathing heavily, Cathy looked around to see if anyone had heard them, but so far she could see no one. Where was that damned key?

She turned back to the door and saw the key hanging above it. Cursing, she took it and quickly opened the lock.

Andor sat in a corner of a hay shed, his face bloody, one eye swollen and the eyebrow above cut.

"Oh, Andor," she whispered and flew to him. "Are you badly hurt?" She cut the ropes binding his arms and legs and helped him stand up. She wrapped her arm around him, got one shoulder under his armpit, and helped him walk to the door.

"I am fine. How did you—" his voice faltered as he saw two armed men lying outside the door.

Cathy bent and picked up both swords, handing them to Andor.

"We must hurry. I sure hope Baldwin got his kitchen waste."

"What?"

The quiet screeching of wheels approached as they rounded the corner. Baldwin's cart was now heaped with vegetable peels and what looked like animal intestines.

From the driver's seat, the old monk glanced at them. "They are having a feast tonight, and she did not have time to throw out the waste from two days ago yet. You are in luck. There is just space for one of you, though. I suggest the Norseman. You, boy, can ride with me. You look Saxon enough. Get in."

CHAPTER TWENTY-ONE

January **26, 878 AD**

"You should not have done that," Andor said.

He was washing the rotting vegetables and intestines off himself, standing up to his chest in the icy water of the lake they had encountered in the early morning.

"What?" Cathy said.

She stood on the shoreline and watched him with a guilty expression. Small mercy at least.

"You should not have come for me," he said through his teeth, barely containing his anger. It was good that he was in the cool water.

"Oh, don't be like that, Andor. I'd never have left you. They wanted to execute you."

"Maybe they should have." He rubbed the beetroot peels off his biceps with water.

She paled. "What?"

He stopped and looked at her. "Maybe you should have let them."

She shook her head. "Andor, come on. You can't be serious."

"Would have been better."

"You need to stop with this nonsense."

"If anything had happened to you because of me—again..."

"I'm fine! Look at me. I found Baldwin. I knocked down two guys. We are out, both alive."

"But it could have been different."

"Isn't it good that you trained me to fight with a sword then?"

Stubborn woman. Andor growled in helpless rage, but it seemed he would not be able to persuade her otherwise.

He took a lungful of air and plunged down into the water. When he emerged, he walked towards the shore and watched with satisfaction as Cathy's lips parted while she took him in.

"See something you like?" he asked, wiping his body with a piece of cloth that Baldwin had given to Cathy along with some food before leaving them. He had also told them that there were just five days of road to Jorvik.

Cathy quickly glanced away. "Sorry. I didn't mean to stare. Your clothes need to dry, so here." She gave him her cloak, and he wrapped himself in it. His skin burned, the air feeling hot after the shock of being in icy water. But he accepted the cloak and walked with her to the campfire.

When they had settled, he shook his head like a dog to get the water off of his hair. Cathy brushed the drops from her cheek, then removed her cap, revealing a bruise by her hairline. Anger at himself flared and his jaw muscles tightened.

"Why did you risk your life to save me?" he said. "You could have gone to Jorvik alone. You must save your Brad. Why risk his life to save mine?"

Cathy looked into the fire. "It was just a good opportunity to test my sword-fighting skills," she said, and Andor's gut twisted with disappointment.

What was he hoping to hear?

That she cared. That she had saved him because he was more important than his twin from the future.

That she wanted to stay.

But he knew the end of their journey together was near.

"Tell me the truth," he said.

She swallowed and flashed a smile. "You know why I saved you."

"Indeed, I do not."

"Because you would have done the same thing, Andor. In fact, you did. At the pagan sacrifice. I owed you."

She owed him. This was true, but not the response he was secretly hoping for.

No matter. This was for the best. He did not deserve her affection. Not after the way he had treated her, and not when Svana's memory deserved his full devotion. The devotion he had been ignoring, replacing with feelings towards Cathy.

This was better. They would arrive in Jorvik, she would be on her way, and he—

He what? Would continue his miserable existence, raiding and fighting and sending the spoils to Svana's family? Ignoring the sucking wound in the pit of his stomach?

Would there never be an end to it?

Andor tugged the cloak tighter as the cold air stabbed his skin from all sides.

"You fought well," he said. "You impressed me. Two men. You have a warrior within you."

A broad smile spread her lips, and she hid her face. "I'd have fought a whole army for you," she said without looking at him. Then she bit her lower lip as though she had said too much.

Something thumped hard in Andor's chest. Maybe it was his heart, or maybe the ghosts were banging at the door because they, too, heard her words.

He knew now that he did not need to worry about protecting her. She had everything she needed to be fine on her own. She was capable of being a help to him, fighting by his side, and even saving him.

If she stayed, he would not need to worry for her life...

"I would have fought a whole army for you, too," Andor said.

Her eyes met his, and he sank into them as if they were a bottomless sea. The need for her returned and heated his veins, and he fought the urge to touch her, to draw her to him, to kiss her.

And suddenly, Andor wished that those five days until they reached Jorvik would stretch to a lifetime.

CHAPTER TWENTY-TWO

The fires of the watchtowers lit the night sky.

"Jorvik," Andor said.

The end was almost here. Cathy's stomach twisted, and she took one step closer to Andor. He walked by her side as he had since they had started this journey together.

Did it have to end? Cathy was torn inside, as though a long, deep chasm formed within her, and it hurt. She needed to think of Brad. He needed her. But how could she leave Andor?

The whitish-gray walls grew ever closer. It didn't look like a wooden fortress. These were thick city walls, about thirteen feet high. Andor stared at the walls as though they were his personal enemy.

At the gates, he announced: "Jarl Andor Thornsson. This woman accompanies me."

"It's Jarl Andor!" the guard yelled. "Jarl, it is me, Anarr. We were worried you were dead. Fridstein wanted to look for you."

"Just let us in," Andor said.

The gates opened and they walked in. Cathy's heart thumped in her ears.

This was it. York.

Three weeks on the road. Fighting with swords, eating meat, washing in icy water, escaping a cult—all for this.

Cathy should find the witch immediately and see if the woman knew how Cathy could get home to Brad. That was what all of this had been about. So why did her legs refuse to take a step away from Andor? Why could she not bring herself to open her mouth? Why were her mind and heart aching to stay?

It was as though some invisible material now connected Cathy and Andor, as though living tissue had grown in the space between them. She could sense his pulse and hear his breath. Separating would be like cutting that flesh.

Inside the walls, York was a big settlement. Some houses were made of stone, but others were built from wattle and timber, with thatched roofs. They stood very close together. The town smelled of animals, food, and wet dirt. Dishes clunked, voices spoke, babies cried, people sang and laughed.

Occasional torches illuminated the streets. They passed by what were clearly the houses of craftsmen, with heavy tools outside, tables and benches where they probably put out goods during the day. Wattled fences separated the longhouses. There were no windows anywhere, and smoke rose from small holes in the roofs. The Anglo-Saxon, Roman, and Viking tangled together here in a strange mixture of styles and history, and—somehow—it worked.

Andor stopped in front of one of the longhouses with a thatched roof, built on timber posts with wattle walls, like many other buildings here. Cathy had thought the house would be empty in his absence, but he bellowed, and men flooded out to greet him, clapping him on the shoulders, hugging him. They glanced curiously at Cathy.

"Guthrum will want to see you tomorrow," one of them said.

When they were done, Andor turned and looked at her. She expected to see relief on his face—he was finally with his people. Safe.

But his lips were tightly pursed, and his eyes were hard. Haunted. "It is late, Cathy," he said. "It is best you see the witch tomorrow."

His voice was husky and low, and there was an edge of vulnerability in it. Cathy's pulse accelerated. "I can spare a night."

The truth was, she was not ready to leave even if he had insisted. But was it because she'd leave the living, breathing, talking representation of Brad in order to go back to the shadow of her fiancé?

She honestly didn't know.

The thought terrified her, twisting in the pit of her stomach. Even one night could make the difference between Brad living and dying. Was she so selfish, so ready to risk Brad's life to be with Andor? It had already been a week longer than Eric had given her before he planned to take measures to cut off Brad's life support.

Just one night, please. Just please, stay alive a little longer.

And if she got back tomorrow and discovered that he was gone, she'd need to live with the guilt for the rest of her life. But one last night with Andor was worth it. In this moment, there was no force in the universe strong enough to make her leave him. Going now would be like cutting out a part of her heart.

When they entered, a squall of laughter thundered around them. A group of men sat drinking and eating around a fire in the long hearth that occupied the middle of the room. A couple of female servants carried food and drinks, cleaned and bustled about the space.

"What is there to laugh about without me?" Andor rumbled, and they looked at him, silent.

An older but muscular man with white hair and an equally snowy beard was especially touched. His eyes widened, and he stiffened but then walked towards Andor like a wooden figure on unbending legs.

He grasped Andor's shoulders with both of his hands. "You are alive, thank Odin," he whispered and pulled Andor into a bear hug.

"Fridstein, you old sea dog," Andor responded warmly and clapped the man on his back loudly. The others came rushing, and each had his own share of claps and hugs, and Cathy found herself smiling from ear to ear. Warmth spread in her chest from seeing Andor so well loved and accepted within his community. She had never felt that back in LA, not even in her yoga community. The only person who had ever given her that feeling was Brad.

Brad.

The warmth inside her was replaced with a stab of guilt. She owed it to him to get back and to see that he got the best chance he could to live.

"How did you survive, you lucky mountain troll?" Fridstein said.

Andor glanced at Cathy, his eyes a warm liquid indigo in the semidarkness of the room. "She was the one who saved me," Andor said, and his words turned her insides into hot lava, melting her hips and knees, filling her feet with lead, welding them to the ground.

They all looked at her.

"Is that a woman?" asked Fridstein.

Cathy removed the cap. She supposed she did not need it.

"A shield-maiden?" Fridstein said, looking her over again with sharper eyes.

"A shield-maiden," Andor said.

"My name is Cathy." She stretched her hand out for Fridstein to shake, but he looked at it as though she was giving him her foot. She withdrew the hand and bowed curtly instead, not sure if she was doing the right thing. "Pleased to meet you."

One corner of Fridstein's mouth curled up. "Pleasure is mine, maiden," he said. "Look at you. You are almost as tall as our Andor."

There was a hint of pride and approval in his voice, and the warm feeling inside Cathy's chest returned. He exchanged a glance with Andor, whose jaw tightened.

"Cannot imagine anyone better to save his arse. Looks like you can hold your own, Cathy."

The rest of the men grunted in approval.

"She is tired," Andor said, taking Cathy's arm and leading her to the other end of the house.

"Wait, let us drink with her. Cathy, stay, tell us about yourself," Fridstein called after her, but Andor dragged her so fast she didn't even have a chance to respond. She'd love to stay and talk to them; they seemed to have accepted her so warmly.

Andor took her through a thin door into what looked like a bedroom. There was a wooden double bed with a beautifully carved headboard. The bed was full of furs, the walls covered with swords and axes and shields. Behind them a door opened, and two servant women came in, one with a bucket, another with firewood.

"Hot coals for your hearth, Jarl," she said and put the coals into the round hearth standing in the middle of the room. "The bathhouse will be ready soon."

The other one added the firewood, then both retreated,

throwing curious glances at Cathy. The room began filling with warm firelight. Cathy should have rejoiced that she would finally sleep in a warm room, in a bed, under a roof, but her mouth went dry as her eyes met Andor's dark, predatory ones. The air disappeared from the room.

"I—" she said. "I wanted to talk to your friends. They seemed nice."

They were the opposite of Brad's friends. They seemed to approve of her even before they talked to her. How crazy was that?

But the way they behaved with Andor, it looked like they loved him. It was the same with those who loved Brad, too.

One corner of his mouth twitched. "*Nice,*" he said, "is certainly not what they are. I do not want to fight my brothers because of a beautiful woman the first night I come back."

She had heard him right, hadn't she? Did he think his friends would find her beautiful, too?

He seemed to. She licked her lips, deciding to let it go, afraid to spook him.

"So—" she said and glanced at the bed. "This is where you sleep."

"This is where *you* sleep," he said. "You must be tired. A hot bath?"

Cathy gazed at him, wide-eyed. "Oh, Andor, you have no idea what those words mean to me."

His eyes darkened, filling with liquid heat. "Take the first turn."

Did he mean he wanted her to wash alone and to sleep alone? She couldn't possibly leave without being with him one last time. They hadn't touched each other after Aethelwulf's fortress. Should she just invite him?

"I—" said Cathy, but the door opened, and a servant girl poked her head into the room.

"The bathhouse is hot, Jarl."

Cathy watched him, her heart beating so hard against her ribcage, it might move her tunic. He held Cathy's gaze for a long time, then looked away.

"Show Cathy where it is. I will wash afterwards."

"Yes, Jarl."

Andor turned his back to her and began undressing. Feeling dismissed, Cathy walked out, disappointment and hurt clawing at her heart.

CHAPTER TWENTY-THREE

ANDOR OPENED the door of the bathhouse. The room smelled like fresh linen, damp wood, and hot stones. Inside, through clouds of steam that rose from the small mound of stones, he saw the full-bodied, long-legged, golden-haired woman the sight of whom made his heart ache and his blood simmer.

She froze, one foot on the bench, leg bent at the knee as she poured water over it, washing the soap away. The seductive pose made him want to sit right there, under her, and help her wash the sweetest spot of her body.

Her skin glistened with water, her hair in thick, wet locks spread across her shoulders and back. Her stomach had a soft curve to it that he wanted to trace his lips along. Her gorgeous arse was a combination of muscle and flesh under flawless skin that made him hard. The lower curve of her breast, full and delicious, peeked from behind her arm, and made his mouth water.

She watched him, love and hope in her soft gray eyes. Her cheeks were flushed—from the heat of the bathhouse, or maybe because of him. Without a word, he began undressing, and watched with satisfaction as her full lips parted and she straightened, the washing cloth still in her hands.

When he had undressed, he walked towards her, his loins aching, and stood before her, inhaling her clean, delicious scent.

The scent he would never experience again after the sun rose.

He clenched his jaw and chased the thought away. The ghosts stood silent behind the door. Where were they when he needed them?

He lifted his hand and traced one knuckle over her cheek, and she closed her eyes, leaning into the touch slightly.

"No tomorrow," he said, and she looked at him. "No yesterday."

Her eyes watered slightly. "No Brad," she said.

"No Svana," he murmured. "No ghosts."

"Just you. And me."

Slowly, he lowered his head and kissed her, his tongue diving into the plush depth of her mouth. She met him with tenderness, softness, and he sank into her, surrounded by her, as if he were sinking into a hot, bubbling spring, the sensations taking over his whole body at once.

Time stopped as he kissed her. The whirlpool of pleasure swirled faster and faster within him. Then she ended the kiss and murmured, "I want to wash you."

Bewildered, he asked. "What?"

"Wash you. I'm clean. I want to care for you."

He spread his arms. "I am at your disposal."

She smiled and sank the cloth into the bucket of warm water, rinsed it, then took a cake of soap smelling of sage, honey, and rosehip and foamed it in her hands. Placing her hands on his chest, she smoothed the foam over his skin. Sweet pleasure spread through him at her touch. He wanted to close his eyes to enjoy it even more, but he did not want to miss a moment of looking at her. He took in her beauty, every movement of her lips, the way her eyes changed as her thoughts changed, the way the water glistened on her skin in the dim light of the hearth and the candles.

The way her face was so loving and caring. He did not want to miss seeing that face for all the gold of nine worlds of Yggdrasil. He wanted to believe that her heart was full of that love, too.

She massaged first his chest, then his stomach, and as her hands moved down, the aching skin of his loins burned hotter the closer she got to his erection. He groaned as she spread the soap on the lower part of his stomach and withdrew.

"Please, go on," he said.

With a sly little smile, Cathy foamed the soap between her hands again and began washing his shoulder, massaging down his arm, and his muscles turned into melting butter. "Oh, you really want to wash me," he said, his head falling back. "I thought you meant—"

Cathy was now at his hand and she even washed between his fingers, massaging his palm with just the right amount of strength to soften the tense muscles and spill relaxation through him.

"Just so that you know," he said. "I will not let you out of here until you are mine at least three times."

She chuckled softly and repeated the process with his other shoulder and arm, then foamed her hands again and went behind him and lathered his back, from his neck to his buttocks and then lower.

No one had ever *massaged* him. The sensation was strange but pleasant. All too soon, she lowered herself to wash his legs, and he tensed in anticipation every time her fingers came close to his throbbing cock. But she never touched it, sly vixen.

She stood up and led him to sit on the wooden bench. She positioned herself behind him and began washing his head, her fingertips doing wonders with his scalp. She poured the warm water over him with a large ladle, helping with one hand to remove the soap from his body. She even gently washed his face and beard with the cloth, finishing with a playful peck on the tip of his nose. He couldn't help but smile back.

Then she finally knelt before him to wash the only part of his body that she still had not touched.

"Just so that you know," she said, gazing up at him from below, so seductive, so beautiful. "I am not letting you out of here until you are thoroughly cleaned."

"You have been very missed."

She hid a smile and looked right at his erection, which twitched in anticipation. She lathered her hands and lay them on him, and that first light touch spread through him like the sweetness of honey, and the buzz of mead, and the warmth of sunlight, and everything else that was delicious and pleasurable in this world.

Cathy massaged his stiff cock, and he groaned, his fingers clenching around the edge of the bench.

Oh, those hands...

Then she washed the soap off him with warm, aromatic water. And then, out of nowhere, her mouth was on him. Her lips encircled him, her tongue sliding around him, bringing him into a sweet, deep sea of silky agony. Her mouth moved along his length, together with her tongue, turning Andor into fluid iron, ringing the tune of the gods.

"Stop, Cathy—" he groaned. "I will—"

"Hmm," she murmured against him, but ignored him and sped up her movements.

She opened her mouth so that he hit so deep against her

throat that he was all within her, and he could not stop himself.

He came, violently, holding onto her shoulders, flying high, rocking on the waves of the pleasure that went through him like a storm.

When he opened his eyes, she was on his lap, pressed against him, her legs on either side of his hips.

He stroked her smooth back, which was now dry.

"That did not count as one of the three times," he said.

She smiled. "It counted as one of the times I made you mine."

He chuckled. "I am already yours. I have been since the moment I saw you. I will always be."

He bit his tongue then as he saw surprise and hope mixed with pain in her eyes. He should not have said that, even though it was true.

"It's a good thing we decided there is no tomorrow. Because if there was a tomorrow, I'd ask you what does that mean—"

He gently put a finger over her mouth. "There is no tomorrow. No ghosts. No betrothed. No dead wives. And no questions. There's you and there's me. And now you will be mine."

As he kissed her, he knew that no matter how much he tried to lose himself in her, the sky above them would soon brighten, the new day would begin, and he'd lose her forever. But for this moment, she was his, and if he could, he would make it last an eternity.

CHAPTER TWENTY-FOUR

January 31, 878 AD

Andor's hand wrapped around Cathy's warmed her skin. He didn't let her hand go all the way through the town as they walked to the witch. They hadn't said more than a few words to each other since last night, which had been the most sensual night of Cathy's life. They'd spent it in gentle lovemaking, saying everything they wanted to say with their bodies.

And now, Cathy wanted every step she took to last forever, pushing off the moment she knew was coming. The time when she'd need to go. She savored the feel of Andor's skin against hers, the warmth of his body next to hers. The very air she breathed seemed to be filled with wonder. Cathy floated beside him, her body both heavy and light after the sleepless night.

How could she leave him?

How could she have betrayed Brad like she had?

Both questions spun in her head, fought in her heart, tearing her apart, spoiling her last moments with Andor.

She couldn't live with herself if she abandoned Brad.

But she also didn't know how to live in a world where Andor did not exist.

They entered the house, which was a regular thatched building. Inside, chickens and geese occupied a stall built with wattled fences. At the hearth sat four children of different ages, the older girls peeling parsnips. A woman in her mid-thirties was spinning wool and singing a song.

In a smithy, quiet smithy
A silent smith goes tonk, tonk, tonk
In a smithy, ashen smithy
Völundr forges death—

She looked up at Cathy and Andor and stopped spinning. "Jarl Andor! Happy and healthy. You two are a curious couple."

Her hair was dark, her eyes a warm brown. She was a pleasant-looking woman, small and friendly. Cathy had expected to meet an older woman, like the Norn, or the universal image of a witch with gray hair falling in tangles. But her eyes didn't pierce Cathy or make her feel as though she was in the presence of someone with supernatural powers, like the Norn. On the contrary, she looked inviting and open.

"Happy and healthy," Andor said and bowed a little. "Ljota, meet Cathy."

Ljota studied Cathy carefully, and warmth spread through her.

"You came from afar," Ljota said.

She stood up and put the spindle—which was wooden and had no carvings on it, to Cathy's disappointment—on the chair.

"Yes, you could say that. I'm from the future."

Ljota crossed her arms and grinned as though Cathy had just told her the best gossip she had heard in years. "From the future? That is far. How did you travel through time?"

Cathy told Ljota what happened with the Norn, omitting the situation with Brad. She did not even want to mention his name in Andor's presence.

"And now I—"

Andor's hand around her fingers twitched, and he let go of her as though her skin burned him.

"And now I must go back," Cathy finished, rubbing the palm he had released. "Andor said you can help. Can you?"

Ljota laughed. "Dear, there are no golden spindles here." She shrugged. "I am no Norn. I am a wife and a mother. I see things, sometimes. I am a good healer. I can talk to the gods and ask them for things—small things, like a good summer, or to protect my husband when he goes raiding. So they all think I'm some sort of a witch. I do not know how you can travel back in time."

A tremor went through Cathy, both relief and desperation. If she had no way of going back home, she'd stay with Andor. She wouldn't need to make the choice to leave him. The thought filled every cell of her being with bubbles, and energy coiled upwards around her spine.

She looked at him, and if her eyes didn't betray her, she saw the same reaction in him—relief and, well, fear.

He was probably still afraid of the internal ghosts that had been haunting him this whole time.

She could relate. Brad's ghost was haunting her, too. Through Brad's familiar face, Andor's sad eyes looked at her.

"But I have a thought," Ljota said.

Cathy's stomach sank. "A thought?"

"Yes. A possible solution. I have heard stories—seen

visions—of this happening already. There were others before you who traveled in time. If we had a sacred grove here, with a rune stone, that would work. But we do not, not yet. So you need to find a place where the stones are saturated with the ancient magic of life and death, as they are in a sacred grove. You could write runes on them and perhaps travel in time."

Cathy swallowed. "Really?"

Ljota shrugged. "This is just a thought. You could try. If you truly want to go back, that is."

Andor's gaze fell heavily on her. "Do you truly want to go back?" he asked.

Cathy's throat clenched till it ached. "I must, Andor. I cannot leave him to die."

"But you can leave me? Even almost dead, he is still more important to you than me, is he not?"

Cathy's stomach dropped, but before she could answer, Ljota intervened.

"No, no, no. There will be none of this talk in my house in front of my children. Here." She took a thin wooden plank and a piece of coal and wrote something on it. "These are the runes you must write on the rock. Any ancient rock on a burial mound should do. There is one near Jorvik, so that is your best chance. Good luck."

She was practically shooing them out of her house. When they were outside, Cathy stared at the plank with the runes, which sent tingles through her fingers. She looked at Andor, whose expression was as dark as the clouds above them.

"Will you help me find that mound?" she asked.

He held her gaze, his eyes so heavy Cathy felt pinned in place.

"Please, Andor."

"No."

CHAPTER TWENTY-FIVE

"You're refusing to help me?" Cathy said, her eyes big.

Andor ground his teeth. Watching her in pain because of him was like stabbing himself in the heart, but he would rather be eaten alive by a forest troll than hand her, like a danegeld, to another man. "I am not going to help you go back to your betrothed," he grated out and walked away from her.

She followed him. "You helped me get all the way here. You brought me to Ljota. How is this different?"

He walked fast through the narrow streets, evading traders, villagers, animals, and carts. Cathy hurried after him.

"It is different," he threw back.

"How?"

He breathed fast, even though he was trying to calm down. He should not think about it. He should not explain to her. He could not even say it out loud, not with Svana's memory banging against the door.

The door that was getting thinner and thinner.

"You know how," he said.

She caught him by the arm and whirled him around to face her. "I don't! Tell me."

"You cannot expect me to help you forever. The agreement was that I deliver you to Jorvik, to the witch. I have honored the agreement. If you want to go back now"—his voice stumbled, choked by a spasm in his throat, and the muscles under his eyes tightened—"I shall not stop you."

People walked around them. They were now in the middle of the busy market square, the scents of food and drink mingling with leather and wet earth. Dozens of voices rang around them, along with horses neighing, goats bleating, and geese cackling. Their eyes locked, Cathy's as gray as the winter sky above them. Her blonde hair was braided around her face, the rest falling in golden locks. She was now in his clean clothes, which hung on her as if she was a scarecrow, but she'd put his broad belt around her waist, and it hugged her, showing her figure. She could not look any more like a warrior queen, with a sword on her hip.

Andor's chest tightened. "You can protect yourself now. Haven't you been trying to get back to Brad these past few weeks? So go. I am not stopping you."

"I—"

"Do you not want to go?" he asked, hope flickering in the bottom of his heart.

She licked her lips. "I don't know, Andor."

A muscle between his eyebrows jerked. "So, you might want to stay?"

She swallowed. "I don't know. Maybe."

He felt lighter. A maybe was not a no.

"Do you want me to stay?" she asked. "I thought you did not want anyone."

She was right. The ghosts began banging at the door, right

on time. *If she stays for you and dies because you failed to protect her, again, there will be no escape for you. Madness will be your end.*

"I do not want to be responsible for anyone. I cannot protect you."

In truth, he knew that she no longer needed his protection, that she was truly a shield-maiden with the spirit of a Valkyrie, fiercer and stronger than she realized.

"But even if you stayed, Cathy, I can never be with you."

Her eyes filled with tears. "Because you still love Svana?"

The town buzzed around him, but all he could see was her. "No," he said.

"Do you love me?" she asked, her voice barely audible.

"Yes." His heart beat like a drum against his ribs.

"Then why?"

"Because my heart is still filled with ghosts of those who died because of me. And they always remind me that I fail to protect those I love."

A tear crawled down her cheek. "Those ghosts, Andor," she said. "I know them. They echo in me, too."

He nodded. "I know they do, Cathy. But that is not even the main reason. Even more important is, if you look at me, can you in all honesty say that you see me? That you love me? That you want to be with me and not your betrothed back home?"

Her eyes widened and she paled, then took a step back, blinking. "What?" her voice came out like a croak.

"Do you want to stay with me? Or am I just the living image of the man you really love? Brad."

She licked her lips, looking at him long and hard. And even before she answered, Andor knew that he had hit the target.

"I don't know," she said.

Andor swallowed and nodded. "That is what I thought, Cathy. I live with my ghosts every day of my life. But I do not want to become one for you."

Cathy's eyes stung, and her heart hurt as though a needle was piercing it.

He thought she was still in love with Brad.

And when she looked at him, she did not know if he was wrong. He looked just like Brad, but a more muscular version of him, and not as tanned.

Her heart, her soul, her body, were reaching for Andor, and only for him, but her mind—

Her mind was confused.

Hurt.

"You're right," she said. "You should not become a ghost, Andor. But, so that you know, you are well on the way."

He frowned. "What?"

"You're becoming a ghost yourself. Your life is an escape. All you do is run away, terrified of the one thing you really must do."

He stood like a mountain above her, yet his eyes showed his pain, the depth of his despair, the expanse of his fear.

"What must I do, Cathy?" he asked, his voice a low rasp.

"Forgive yourself."

He jerked and turned away. "You do not know what you are talking about."

"Maybe not," she said. "But I know a coward when I see one—the mirror has shown me enough times. You are running away again. And until you can forgive yourself, you will never live a full life. Well, any life for that matter."

He looked at her, his chin high, his eyes dark, his nostrils flared. "Maybe that is exactly the destiny that I deserve."

She swallowed and shook her head. "It isn't, Andor. Ask yourself this. If it was reversed, and you died because Svana failed to come back in time, would you have wanted her to move on with her life or would you want her to live like this, crippled by guilt, all the life sucked out of her? If you loved her, what would you wish for her?"

Andor grimaced, his face a tight mask of disgust and anger, and his eyes glistened with pain.

"I would never want her to live a crippled life, because she would have always kept her word to me. And I did not."

Cathy shook her head.

"So. Here we are. A ghost and the time traveler who loves him."

Andor's fists clenched.

Cathy looked around. "I must go. Maybe I can ask Fridstein to take me to the mound."

"Be my guest."

She held his gaze for the last time, her whole body hurting at the thought of leaving him, as though he was a part of her body that was being torn away.

"Goodbye, Andor," she said.

Without waiting for his answer, she turned and walked away.

"Goodbye, Cathy," she thought she heard him say, and she sped up, tears filling her eyes, and began running, before she could turn back to him and beg him to take her back.

CHAPTER TWENTY-SIX

Los Angeles, January 31, 2019

Waves crashed against the shore. The sound was familiar and calmed Cathy down, relieving the tension in her chest and allowing her to suck in air. Cold, wet. People's voices. Gray light seeped through her closed eyelids.

Where was she? England?

She hadn't heard the sound of waves in weeks.

With a jerk, she sat up and opened her eyes, squinting from the brightness. The sun was brilliant in the blue sky and reflected against the ocean, almost blinding her.

Palm trees. Rough, low rocks of the California shoreline. Some people surfed the waves while others chilled on the beach.

Pain rolled over her, crushing her heart, stealing her breath, her fingers clutching and gathering sand in her fists.

She had left Andor.

Fridstein had taken her to the mound. She had drawn the runes on the rock and then put her hands on it.

And it had worked.

Now she was here. And Andor was hundreds of years in the past. He didn't even exist in this world. She felt so heavy she couldn't move a digit.

Tears welled in her eyes as she looked around and struggled to stand, her head spinning, the ground sinking under her shoes. She straightened slowly, put her chin on her chest, closed her eyes, and took several long, deep breaths.

When her head stopped spinning, she looked down at herself. She was still dressed like a Viking, the sword on her hip.

What now?

She was here. She had come for Brad, so she had to go to him and make sure he was still alive and that no one was trying to switch off his machines.

If Andor was right, and she loved Brad and not him, why did her chest hurt as though a bomb had exploded and shredded it to pieces?

She walked up the beach towards the path leading to the road. She should maybe find a horse or just walk—

Wait. What horse? Walking would be crazy. She was back in the modern world and she owned a car for god's sake. At least she had before she'd traveled in time. How much time had passed? Was her car even there? Stolen or towed? Were people looking for her or did they think she'd drowned?

Her car would be useless even if it was still here, because she didn't have her keys or her phone.

She looked around and saw surfers walking up the path. Maybe they would give her a lift, but she needed to do something about the sword first, and her clothes... She was so used to the sword by now she'd feel naked without it, but she couldn't go around LA with it. She hid it behind some big rocks near the path. It was hard enough to get a lift here under normal circumstances, but the way she was dressed was going to make it impossible. Unless—

If she took off her pants. Andor's tunic reached her mid-thigh, at least as long as the dresses a lot of women wore these days. And his boots were tall and looked really badass.

Cathy wondered where her old self had gone, the one who would never assume the local surfers would help her and who would get totally self-conscious about showing her legs or her curves. Now she was in warrior mode; she had a target and there were no obstacles that would stop her.

Besides, she didn't feel self-conscious about her body anymore. Instead, she took it as it was: tall and strong.

And beautiful.

Hmm. That was new.

Cathy took off the pants, tucking them in around the sword, and walked up the hill to the parking lot. When she got there, surprisingly, the car was still parked where she'd left it, and she patted it as she passed by.

In the parking lot, the surfers were loading their boards on their cars, and Cathy hurried towards them. She scanned the group and spotted Jason—no Miranda.

"Hey, Jason!" Cathy cried as she hurried towards the group.

Jason turned around and his eyes widened. "Cathy? What are you doing here?"

"I like your vintage dress," said a girl Cathy had seen before on the beach. If Cathy was right, the girl sounded sincere, maybe even a little envious.

"Thanks," Cathy mumbled. That must have been the first compliment she'd ever gotten from the group. "Jason, I need your help. Please."

He glanced at the two friends who were getting a ride with

him, but they said nothing and just frowned at her. "What is it?" he asked.

"I lost my car keys and my phone, and I need to get to Brad's hospital right now. Please, can you take me there? For him?"

Jason glanced back at his friends. "Sorry, guys, I'm taking her. If you want to go home with someone else, I'm sure Ollie and Lance can take you."

The girl who'd just complimented her said, "No, it's fine. I don't mind."

Cathy beamed. She couldn't believe they were so open to helping her. Something was different about this version of home. "Thank you, guys."

During the ride, Cathy found out that it was January thirty-first. She had been away for about three weeks—the same amount of time that had passed in the Viking Age. But whether Brad was still on life support or not, they didn't know. What if his parents had switched it off?

When they arrived, Cathy hurried directly to Brad's room, her heart pounding in her ears.

She opened the door, and the acrid scents of illness and antiseptic hit her in the face. The machines still beeped, and Brad's parents stood by his bed, as well as Dr. Gentzelman. Linda had a Kleenex in her hand, pressed against her mouth, tears streaking her face. Eric's arm was around her shoulders, his face a tight, sad mask. They both looked at Brad, who lay in the exact same position she had left him.

His beard had grown, and he was a little paler, a little thinner than she remembered.

He looked so much like Andor. The thought hit her so hard she had to grasp the doorframe.

Dr. Gentzelman checked the clipboard in her hands. "All

right, the court decision looks fine, Mrs. and Mr. Larsen. Whenever you are ready, we'll let him go—"

Cathy felt dizzy. "Let him go?" she croaked.

Their heads turned to her. Linda's eyes widened and Eric frowned. "It is done, Cathy," Linda said through tears, her voice breaking. "It's time."

Cathy walked towards Brad on stiff legs. She sat on the edge of the bed without taking her eyes off him. "You got the court approval?"

"Yes."

She shook her head. "I—"

She wanted to say she wouldn't allow them. That he might still wake up. That they still could fight for his life.

That she needed him. That she couldn't live without him. Without his positivity, the light that he always brought to the room. That she missed his voice, which was always charged with energy. That life with him was fuller. Bigger. Brighter.

Except—

This was no longer true.

She saw it in his pale skin, in his eyes, which didn't move under his eyelashes. She heard it in the beeping of the machine.

He was not coming back.

The realization came crashing over her like a wave in a storm, blinding her, deafening her with an overwhelming force. Her chest tightened, her lungs shrunk to the size of a fist, as though she was sinking, drowning under the surf.

She swallowed several times, panic gripping her, then finally she inhaled with a whelp. They looked at her, worried.

"Can I have a moment with him, please?" Cathy asked, her voice hoarse.

"You aren't going to fight us?" Eric said.

Cathy's eyes blurred from tears, and she only managed to shake her head.

"Thank you," Linda said and squeezed her shoulder.

Cathy caught Linda's hand and squeezed back.

When they were alone, Cathy took Brad's hand in hers. It was so warm, as though he might respond to her touch. And she wanted nothing more.

But he wouldn't respond. She knew that now.

The man who had really loved her for who she was. The man who had showed her what happiness was. The man she had thought she'd spend the rest of her life with.

"You and I," Cathy said, "we always know what to say to each other. But for the last year, I've been the one doing the talking. If I'd listened, I would have heard you. Your silence said everything."

She laid her head on his chest and listened to the weak beat of his heart. She brushed her fingers against the hospital gown and inhaled the scent of it—washed linen and hospital.

Brad didn't even smell like himself anymore.

"I miss you so much I can't breathe." She swallowed a hard knot in her throat.

Her stomach, her chest, her throat clenched as hard as rocks. Her eyes burned.

"But I must let you go," she said.

His dear, handsome face stayed impassive. "I was looking for your spirit in the ocean. I had thought maybe you lost it somewhere out there. That I could find it and bring it back."

She cupped his bearded jaw.

"But instead of your spirit, I found something I never imagined was possible. I traveled back in time, and I met a man. A man who looks just like you. Maybe he's your ancestor from Norway, or maybe it's just a crazy coincidence. Or destiny."

She stroked the side of his face. "I fell in love with him,

Brad. I'm sorry. I'm so sorry if you feel I betrayed you. I really didn't mean to. All I wanted was to return to you and for you to return to me. He helped me, and I'm back here thanks to him. But the life I thought I'd been fighting for is gone. You're not here anymore, and you're never coming back, are you?"

Tears burned her cheeks, but she ignored them.

"Everything good in my life happened because of you. You are the only one who believed in me, you gave me strength, you lifted me up. Even that crazy time travel happened because of you. Even Andor. If you helped me find him, thank you, my love. Maybe I shouldn't talk to you about him, but you are my best friend, and somehow, I feel you're happy for me."

She swallowed the hard knot.

"If you are watching over me from somewhere, thank you. I would do the same for you. And I'm so sorry you had to die because you chose me and because you protected me. I never wanted it to happen. Oh god, how I wish you'd never had that accident. How I wish you hadn't chosen me. You'd be alive now, Brad. But you're not, and I need to do the impossible. I need to let you go."

She studied him, her chest empty. She cried silently and held his hand. When her tears dried up and she knew she couldn't keep him here any longer, she leaned into him and kissed him gently on the side of the lips free of the tube.

"Goodbye, my love," she whispered.

She lingered over him a moment, then stood up and called Eric and Linda back.

"I'm ready," she said.

"Okay, honey," Linda said.

They wrapped their arms around her shoulders, and they stood like a family, saying goodbye to the person they loved. Dr. Gentzelman looked at them and Linda nodded, tears in her eyes.

The doctor removed the tube from Brad's mouth and unplugged the machines. A deafening silence fell over the room. Linda cried without a sound. Cathy watched Brad, savoring every moment, searing his face in her psyche forever.

After a while—minutes or hours, she wasn't sure—Dr. Gentzelman felt his pulse and listened to his heart. "Time of death, 4:28 PM. I'm very sorry."

Even though a part of Cathy went forever with Brad, strength and confidence straightened her shoulders and filled her chest.

That part was Brad.

CHAPTER TWENTY-SEVEN

Viking Northumbria, February 14, 878 AD

"Here it is." Andor pulled on the reins to stop his horse.

Fridstein reined in next to him. "Looks like a good, rich farm. You have not seen them since two winters?"

The air was wet and crisp, and Andor's body was pleasantly tired after half a day's ride.

His fists clenched tighter. "Yes."

Below them lay a sloping valley, flanked by a thick forest on one side and dark, rolling hills on the other. On the hilltop stood a large farm with five buildings, including a house, a barn, two storage buildings, and a workshop for smithing and carpentry. Wind whispered through the bare branches of the trees, but otherwise the farm was quiet.

Because Ubba had granted him the land, Andor knew the farm had already been here and had a few buildings ready to be worked and lived in. He had given the land to Harek and Nanna, Svana's parents. They had moved in here with Svana's sister Ilmr, her husband, and their children. They now had several servants and slaves who lived in the other buildings.

It was good land, a rich beginning for a new life, and based on the neatness of the buildings, the state of the roofs and walls, it looked like they were doing well with it.

Andor sent a trusted servant here regularly with silver and treasure from his conquests. It was like paying a danegeld for a failure for which he could not forgive himself.

But silver and gold could not buy him that forgiveness. Cathy was right. He had heard her voice, the last words she had said to him every day since she had left. "Would you have wanted her to move on with her life or would you want her to live like this, crippled by guilt, all the life sucked out of her?"

With Cathy's absence, it was as though the air had stopped nourishing his lungs, as though the sun had sunk and would never come up again. As though Ragnarok, the end of the world, was near.

And now he had come here to—

He did not quite know. He knew he could not live another day without seeing Svana's parents.

He had brought silver as a pretense to see them. Fridstein had insisted on coming with him.

Andor needed to look into the eyes of the parents whose daughter had died because of him, something he had never done after her death. He had avoided looking at them. He had run away from them, buying their forgiveness with this land and his silver.

But ever since Cathy had left, her words had nagged at him, and the door that he had shut had begun lurching.

He needed to look them in the eye and say that he was sorry.

"Come on," Andor said, spurring his horse to let it run towards the buildings.

Even before they arrived, the door to the main longhouse opened, and Harek came out, his eyes wide.

"Andor," he said. "Son."

Harek was a sturdy man, his hair still dark, although gray was beginning to show at his temples.

"Harek." Andor glanced at him but could not look for more than a moment. He jumped off the horse and stood by it like a carved statue, unable to move any closer.

"Come in, you and Fridstein," Harek said and gestured to the entrance of the longhouse. "The new ale must be ready by now."

Andor gave a curt nod of thanks, and he and Fridstein tied their horses by the drinking pit.

Inside, the whole farm was there. Nanna and Ilmr sewed, while servants cooked food and occupied children. Both women's hands stilled as they saw Andor.

"Andor," Nanna said, then her face crumpled and she began crying. Ilmr hugged her and rubbed her shoulder.

Andor's jaw tightened so much he thought he might break it. His ghosts were not behind the door anymore. They were right in front of him, flesh and blood.

"I—" he said. "I should not have come." He turned around and walked out of the house.

Harek followed him. "No, no. She is just— She has not seen you for a while. Do not go."

Andor's face tightened. He turned to Harek but still could not look him in the eyes. "I shall not bother your family."

"We are your family, too."

Andor's lips curved, as tight as ropes. "The family I have ruined."

Silence hung between them, because he had said what he had come to say. He had made the step, and he knew he could not run anymore. All he could do was stay.

Face the ghosts.

With his chest as hard and as cold as an iron cage, as though frozen in a chunk of ice, he raised his eyes to Harek's, meeting them for the first time since Svana died.

Ready for punishment. Ready for judgment. Ready for whatever his father-in-law would give him.

What he saw in them was Svana. He had not even realized before how similar her eyes were to her father's.

And just like in Svana's, there was no hatred, no resentment, and no blame.

Just love.

"You have not ruined your family, Andor," Harek said. "She did not die because of you. She died because of Jarl Elgr. And you avenged her."

Andor swallowed hard. "Did you know that I had promised her I would come earlier? Had I kept my promise, she would be alive. Did you know that, Harek? Do you still think me family now?"

Harek's eyes darkened, blurred by pain. "I did not know that. Why—why did you stay away?"

Andor's arms shook. "Because Ubba asked me to get the jeweled Bible that would be a strong negotiation point for him. Jarl Elgr raided because he knew I'd come back with ships sailing low with silver and spoils after I had given Ubba the book. Had I not stayed, had I not made my name so famous, and had I not chosen my pride over your daughter, she would be alive. So, you see, it is not Jarl Elgr you should blame. It is me."

And then he knew—he needed to have this punishment. Either he would be punished, or he had to forgive himself. And he could not forgive himself. Cathy was right.

He unsheathed his sword and handed it to Harek, handle first. Harek looked at it with a deep frown.

"Take your revenge, Harek," he said. "Take your revenge, because I cannot live like this. Not a day passes that I do not miss her. I came here under the pretense of giving you silver." He shoved the sack with coins and jewelry into Harek's hand. "But in earnest, it was to face you and to tell you the truth. Either you will grant me your punishment or your forgiveness."

Harek's face distorted in a grimace of pain and anger. He took the sword from Andor's hands and held it, breathing heavily, then raised the tip to Andor's neck, the edge digging into his skin.

Andor stood and did not look away. The door inside of him swung wide open. The ghosts broke free. They thundered within him, tearing his soul apart, screaming in his ears, clawing at his throat to be released in a howl.

Harek lowered the sword, his face still distorted. "Is this why you gave us this farm and why you send the silver? Not because you wanted to support us but because you feel guilty?"

Andor could not say anything, his throat and mouth hard as rock.

Harek let the sword go, and it clanked to the ground. "You are right, Andor. You should have chosen her. You should have gone home earlier. And if you had, maybe she would be alive."

His words slashed at Andor like a whip. He closed his eyes. This hurt so much he began to sweat.

"But I forgive you, son," Harek said. "That is what she would have wanted. She would have never wanted you to be haunted by guilt your whole life. She would have wanted you to take revenge against her killers, which you did. But then she would have wanted you to live a full life. To rebuild your home. To find a woman you could be happy with. And to never make such a mistake again."

Andor felt as though soothing rain fell on his scorched skin, extinguishing the fire, calming him. And the ghosts within him silenced, too.

"And you should forgive yourself, as well," Harek said.

Andor looked at him, his eyes gritty. "You do not know what your words mean to me, Harek."

Harek's eyes filled with tears, and he clasped Andor's shoulder and squeezed it. "Come inside, son. Have a meal with us. Let us drink ale and mead and remember Svana. And stop sending us your silver. You do not owe us anything."

Andor gave a curt nod and followed Harek inside. And for the first time since Svana's death, the door was open, the ghosts were silent, and he felt at peace.

And now that he had that, the need for Cathy sucked at the bottom of his stomach. His hands itched to touch her, to have her by his side, to call her his forever. He knew Cathy had been right. Svana did not wish for him to suffer. Svana wished for him to be happy. Svana knew Cathy was the one he could find peace with.

But once again he was too late. Cathy was gone forever.

CHAPTER TWENTY-EIGHT

Sonada Beach, Los Angeles, February 14, 2019

The beach was quiet under the cold winter sun, just the waves crashing into the sand and seagulls screeching. Around a hundred people had arrived for the funeral, as far as Cathy could tell. No one was in black—she had specifically asked people to wear something beachy.

Brad would have wanted that.

Everyone who could surf wore wetsuits, including Cathy. The hot-pink wetsuit Brad had given her was now eleven hundred years back in time, in Wessex. If it survived until today, it would give archaeologists a real puzzle.

But she'd bought a new one just like the one Brad had given her. She thought he'd want colors and joy and that he'd wish everyone to be grateful for their life and their health.

Because they were here, and he was not.

Cathy held the urn with his ashes in her hands as she looked around at the guests. Eric and Linda, her own parents and her sister, as well as Miranda and Jason and the rest of the localists. There were many friends, fellow surfers, and athletes Brad competed with at surfing championships all over the world. Everyone had come to say goodbye.

As Cathy looked at them, gratitude and love filled her, alongside the sadness and the aching emptiness.

Yes, she had been busy with arranging things after Brad's death, and that activity had distracted her a little from the raging, throbbing, acute pain in the middle of her being. She understood now why Andor had run. She was glad to be distracted from missing him. From having lost Brad.

Cathy's fingers brushed the beautiful wooden urn.

"Let's begin," she said as loudly as she could. "Thank you all for coming. Today is Valentine's Day, the day of love. The perfect day to say goodbye to the man who showed me what true love means and followed his heart every day of his life."

The last word made her voice jump a little, but she would not cry again. She'd said her piece to Brad alone, and it was between him and her. Now she was ready, as his partner and his friend, to help other people honor his memory.

She also knew that there was nowhere Brad would rather rest than in the sea.

"Brad Larsen was an extraordinary human being," she said. "He was every woman's dream." She smiled as she looked around at the women in the crowd. "Come on, ladies, it's true." Many chuckled softly, with sadness in their eyes. "But he was mine. He chose me. He loved me. I did not know why for a while. I always looked for a catch, for something to go wrong. But he truly loved me for who I was. I'm sure you all had a similar feeling in his presence—of being appreciated for who you are. That's why he had so many friends, because people enjoyed being in his company, because his affection was unconditional. If Brad wanted to leave a legacy, it would be for everyone to be happy with themselves."

Cathy swallowed, looking into the eyes of every guest in the crowd.

"Live your life embracing who you are. Love yourself—the good, the bad, and the ugly. I think the world has become a darker place without Brad. But if we take even one step closer towards who we really are, it will be brighter."

She smiled and saw people smiling back at her and nodding. She met her mom's eyes, and noticed Mom was crying. So was Miranda. Jason wore a sad smile. Cathy would certainly live her life as a tall, big-boned, California girl— whom she loved.

"I have clung to Brad this past year," Cathy said, "unable to move on without him. But I have finally learned the lesson Brad wanted to teach me. I have learned to love myself, and I am finally ready to let Brad go."

She turned to the ocean and took her surfboard. She walked into the waves, jumping as they lifted her up. Then she lay down on the board and paddled out far enough to ensure all of Brad would stay in the ocean and that the wind would carry him into the waves. She opened the urn and held it above the water.

"Till we meet again, my love," she whispered and tipped the urn over.

The ashes swirled in the air for a moment, the wind carrying some of them away, the rest dissolving, mixing with the power of the ocean. Cathy watched the last of Brad's ashes return to the natural world he loved, and for the first time since his accident, she felt his presence. Maybe it was the wind, or water splashing against the surfboard, but she thought she heard a whispered "thank you" and "I love you."

She smiled gently, feeling the wind kissing her cheek and playing with a lock of her hair.

She stayed out a bit longer, enjoying the peace and quiet, the gentle rocking of the waves and the breeze. When she turned around to paddle back to the shore, she saw an old lady on a surfboard next to her.

Cathy jerked, surprised, and almost fell off the board.

"Oh my gosh!" She put her hand on her heart, which raged against her ribs. "You scared me."

"Hello, dear," the Norn said. "Sorry. I didn't want to interrupt your moment with Brad." She cocked her head and flashed a sweet, motherly smile. "You did so well. You did the right thing."

Cathy studied the woman.

"You sent me back in time," Cathy said. "You're the reason I went on that crazy adventure. You're the reason I learned to sword-fight and lived through several near-death experiences. You're the reason I met Andor." She gripped the cold, wet edges of the surfboard. "The man I love."

The Norn sighed, one corner of her mouth crawling up. "The man you love?"

Cathy nodded. "The man I love."

"How about that? What did I tell you? I knew you two were made for each other."

"Are we?"

"Now the question is, what are you going to do about it?" She leaned forward a little. "Are you ready to follow your heart?"

It was as if she'd hit Cathy in the chest with a log. Her breath whooshed out of her, and she couldn't move. She closed her eyes to gather her strength for a few moments and think about the question.

"Do you mean, you can send me back?" Cathy asked, opening her eyes.

She was alone in the ocean.

When she was back at the beach, her mom and dad came to her, tears in their eyes. Her sister was taking selfies for her Instagram channel.

"Honey," Mom said, "that was so beautiful, what you said about accepting yourself. I was really touched. And good for you for losing all that weight."

Dad hugged her and wanted to say something, but his phone rang, and he picked it up and turned away.

"Mom, I did not lose weight on purpose. It was all the"— she cut herself off from saying hunger, traveling through winter in medieval times, daily sword-fighting training— "exhaustion and the stress of the funeral and arranging Brad's affairs. I really couldn't care less about my weight."

"Well, you always said so, but—"

"But now I mean it. And you should gain some weight, Mom. You would look gorgeous at any size."

Mom opened her mouth slightly, and she was just about to say something when Miranda walked up. Cathy excused herself.

"Hey, Cathy, thank you for this beautiful ceremony and for organizing the funeral," Miranda said. "It couldn't have gone any better."

Cathy smiled and they both turned to the ocean where world-class surfers were now enjoying the waves—together with Brad, no doubt.

"Wow, look at them," Cathy said, admiring the skill of the athletes. They all wore wetsuits of different colors, and their surfboards were all so colorful, as well. "This beach never saw such talent."

Miranda swallowed. "You're right. It never has. Just Brad,

and us. And we're amateurs compared to him. I wish we could see more of that. We can learn so much from them."

Cathy looked at Miranda. "You can stop your bullying and let others onto the beach."

Miranda looked at her feet, then at Cathy. "You're right. We already did, actually. In memory of Brad. If we hadn't chased him away, he'd be alive."

Cathy shook her head and grasped Miranda's shoulder. "Don't blame yourself. I'm sorry if I made you think you were guilty. Your intention wasn't to make him have an accident."

"Still, the beach doesn't belong to us. Everyone should be able to enjoy it and get better at surfing on a safe beach. Maybe we'll see more of that." She pointed at the surfers with her chin.

Cathy smiled. "Great idea."

"Thank you," she said, taking Cathy's hand in hers. "And I'm sorry for your loss."

"Thank you, Miranda."

"I'll go join the world champions." She giggled a little, picked up her surfboard, and ran into the waves.

Cathy sighed, a smile spreading on her face. But after just a minute alone, her chest began throbbing again, as she remembered Andor.

Now that everything was done, Brad was gone, the beach was free, and she did not need anyone's approval but her own... What now?

Cathy hugged herself, lifting her face to the cold sunshine. What now?

Now, she wanted to be with Andor.

Even more than that, she wanted to pick up a sword and sail off on some crazy adventure with him. Or just make love in the middle of winter woods.

She wanted to go back to medieval times.

To the man she loved.

Now that everything was settled here, and her job was done, she knew with every cell of her being that it was not the image of Brad she loved in Andor.

It was the man himself. Rude, arrogant, brave, strong, sarcastic Andor, who never gave her his approval unless she earned it.

And who taught her to seek her own approval within herself.

Andor, who had taught her to be a shield-maiden.

But she had left him. And he had left her, too. He didn't want to be with her—but only because he had thought she loved Brad and not him. But it wasn't true!

What if she told him that she really loved him, that he was the man for her? The man she had crossed hundreds of years for? The man she'd gladly wait for—until he got over Svana's death?

Would he give her a chance then?

Cathy had to try. If there was even the slightest chance, she had to take it or she'd regret it her whole life.

But how would she go back? Could she draw those runes on a rock and travel back in time?

She still remembered the runes. She must go to England, to York, and find that mound!

Her heart thumping in her chest, she ran towards the path away from the beach.

"Cathy!" her mom yelled. "Where are you going?"

"Where I belong."

CHAPTER TWENTY-NINE

Hvaldalen, Norway, May 7, 878 AD

Andor drove the ax into the bare tree trunk lying on the trestles, and then again and again, the muscles of his shoulders and back singing from the joy of work. The skin of his naked torso rejoiced in the warm sunlight, and the gentle breeze cooled him, drying off his sweat. Perfect weather for building. Around him, dozens of axes clinked against wood, hammers banged, men cried out from strain or to coordinate setting a length of timber in the earth or raising beams for the roof.

The new great hall was well underway. The wooden frame stood, and men worked hard to build the first wall. Having the jarl's hall constructed was important for all the people of Hvaldalen. It was the symbol of a fresh start for everyone.

After Andor had returned to Jorvik from Harek and Nanna's farm, he had known he wanted to return home to Hvaldalen. He was ready. The forgiveness he had found there had made him realize he owed it to Svana and the victims of the slaughter to rebuild their home. That was what they would have wanted. Not to bend to the tragedy and run away from the consequences with his tail between his legs, but to stay, to face his responsibility and to accept the death of his and their loved ones.

To start anew.

He knew the dead of the village would wait for him and his people in Valhalla, Odin's hall of the slain, and Fólkvangr, Freyja's fields of the dead.

When he got back to Jorvik, he had called to anyone from Hvaldalen who was in Jorvik to go back home if they wished, telling them he would rebuild their home. Many had chosen to stay because they had already started new lives there, but many new had joined him, too. Of course, his silver and other treasure from countless raids helped, and he could hire builders to come and rebuild the village as quickly as possible.

To thank his people for their loyalty and patience, the first thing Andor did when they arrived was to raise another rune stone for the fallen, right next to Svana's.

Of course, the joy of seeing his home rising again, could not be full without the one person he wanted to share it with.

Cathy.

Andor glanced at Fridstein, who worked on his house together with his wife, and watched with a tightness in his chest that came from both the joy of seeing them together and, if he was honest, a stab of jealousy. The sight reminded him of the loss of both Svana and Cathy, and his whole body ached from the memories. Normally, he would have run away from them, looking for a distraction, but now he closed his eyes and took them in, because in that pain, was also love and the joy of thinking of them both.

At least Cathy must be safe and well, back in her time. Andor had ensured that. He had followed her and Fridstein right away, but not close enough that they would notice him. When he saw Cathy touch that rock and disappear, his world had come crashing down, shaking and crumbling like a rock under Thor's hammer. His gut had twisted until it hurt, pain raging within him.

He'd walked to the rock, surprising Fridstein, whose eyes were as wide as armrings. Andor had inspected the rock and could see the remnants of the runes written with coal dissolve into the stone and disappear.

Well. Somehow this must be for the better. He had told her to go.

He would give anything to see her again now, to touch her, to hear her voice.

But that was impossible, and he needed to learn to live without her. His people needed him. He had to live for them now.

"Look, a ship." Fridstein came to stand next to him and pointed at the fjord.

Andor straightened, the ax still in his hand, and covered his eyes with his other hand to shield them from the sun. Indeed, a single Viking ship cut through the glistening mirrorlike water of the fjord, oars rising and falling.

"Looks like a trading ship," Andor said.

"Another batch of timber?" Fridstein asked.

"No, we have all the timber we need for now."

"It is best we warn the men," Fridstein said. "A new trader wouldn't be coming here hoping for business. Not while everyone in Norway thinks the village is still empty. The news could not have spread so fast."

"Tell the men to take their swords. Let us find out."

While Fridstein called the men, Andor grabbed his sword and strode down the path towards the wooden jetty. The banging and the thumping halted as some of his men followed him while others stood where they were, weapons in hand. Fridstein walked by his right side.

They stood on the jetty and watched the ship approach, and when it was close enough to distinguish individual people, Andor thought he had been blinded.

Among the brown and the gray of the furs on men's shoulders, among the pale yellow of the linen tunics, long golden hair flew in the wind. Then he saw a tall figure dressed in a rich brynja chain mail, with a shield in her hand. A shield-maiden?

She had Cathy's hair and height.

"Do you see that, Fridstein?" Andor asked.

"I do," Fridstein said, and the surprised murmur of the men confirmed the unusual sight. "It's a woman!"

Andor's skin tingled everywhere, even his scalp.

Andor felt Fridstein's eyes on him, but he dared not look away from the ship, afraid that the beautiful vision would disappear.

Could it really be Cathy? Or was he going mad from missing her? His fists clenched, one around the handle of his sword.

"Can this ship crawl any slower?" he growled.

His stomach was so tight he might have a spasm, and his heart beat so loudly, the thumping was all he could hear. Moments stretched into an eternity. He was considering taking a fishing boat and rowing towards the ship himself, just to end his suffering.

And then the vision raised her hand and waved it in quick, broad swipes.

"A Valkyrie," Fridstein murmured in awe.

Andor still could not see her face, but he raised one hand in return, his heart bursting with hope. He was not afraid of ghosts any longer, but oh, he was afraid to hope.

If this turned out to be some mean joke of the gods, he wasn't sure how he'd recover.

The ship glided closer and closer.

"Andor," he heard. "Andor!"

Cathy.

But still he wouldn't believe it until he saw her face.

And then he did.

A smile ear to ear, those sparkling gray eyes, the rosy cheeks, the lush full lips he'd longed to kiss since the first moment he saw them. That beautiful, dear face of the woman he loved.

"Andor!" she screamed again, even jumping up and down a little.

"Is that really Cathy?" Fridstein said.

Andor did not even reply. He walked in a broad stride to the very edge of the jetty, impatient for the ship to dock. He did not see anyone else, though he knew the boat was full. She was his sole focus.

Finally, the ship arrived, and his men took the ropes to dock it, but Cathy did not wait until it was secured. She jumped off the boat and right into his arms.

He caught her, stepping back a little from the powerful impact of her in full iron armor, and sank into her scent—the sun, the sea, and her. She was in his arms, strong and warm, soft and silky.

"Andor," she whispered next to his ear, warming his skin.

He crushed her to himself, afraid if he let her go she would run away again or dissolve into thin air. Then she leaned back a little and their eyes met.

"It is truly you," he said.

"It is truly me. I found you."

He sank in her beautiful eyes, so bright, and sparkling like the waters of a summer sea.

And then he kissed her. He kissed her as though he could not do otherwise, as though he could not take his next breath, as though his heart could not continue to beat if he didn't.

The kiss was gentle and hungry at the same time. The softness of these lips, the silkiness of this tongue, the taste of this mouth. She moaned slightly as he dug his fingers into her hair with one hand and pressed her against him with the other.

She leaned back again and met his gaze, her eyes shiny. "Okay," she whispered, "I'll just get right to it." She paused. "I love you, Andor. I came to say I love you. Not Brad. Not a ghost. You."

His stomach squeezed. The world became brighter, sunnier, the colors richer. Her words reverberated within him, resonating in every bone, in every sinew.

"If you still want me to go, I'll go," she continued. "If you are not ready, I understand. But I let Brad go. We had a funeral, and I knew he would want me to find you. So here I am. Finding you. Staying with you forever. If you'll have me."

His chest burst with joy, every word she said like a healing balm, like water washing away the dust and neglect from his soul.

"Say something," she said, looking at him steadily. "Should I go?"

Andor struggled for breath. Was he ready for this? For her love? For the happiness of a lifetime?

Cathy frowned, watching his face. "You're silent. Should I take this as a no?" She stepped back, out of his arms. "Okay, I'll go."

He would not let her go even if Odin came and laid Valhalla at his feet for her. Finally, he could step into the future he craved and deserved. He caught her hand and pulled her back into his arms, pressing her against him.

"Do not dare move," he said, and her smile sent warmth spreading through his veins.

"You don't want me to go?"

"No."

"You want me to stay?"

"Yes."

She licked her lips, a playful smile on them. "Do you love me?"

He pressed his lips together to hide a smile. She looked at his lips as if enthralled and gently touched them. "You're smiling."

Her touch tickled his skin, and he stopped resisting. "I love you, Cathy."

She produced the most delightful laugh.

"You had me back in Wessex, the moment I saw that bright-pink armor," he said.

She laughed and slapped him lightly on the chest.

"Be my wife. I need a woman by my side to help me rebuild our home."

The humor was gone from her face. "Is that the only reason you want to marry me?"

He chuckled. "Yes."

She slapped him again, harder. "Are you not going to be afraid to leave me here alone?"

"Do you have your strange pink suit with you? All enemies will run at the sight of it."

She laughed, and he joined her.

"But in all earnestness," he said. "I am not afraid to leave you unprotected. You will be a great shield-maiden, and I will help you become one. And I know my life will be in good hands with you."

She kissed him, sending bursts of happiness through his veins.

"I will be your wife," she said. "But only if you give yoga one more shot."

A broad smile spread his lips as happiness filled him like a jug of mead. He said, "Me watching you every morning with your sweet arse up in the air is the only way our marriage will go."

He sealed the deal with a kiss that made him wish to consummate the marriage right then and there.

EPILOGUE

Hᴠᴀʟᴅᴀʟᴇɴ, September 15, 878 AD

"Now, ᴛᴜʀɴ ɪɴᴡᴀʀᴅ," the sweetest voice in the world instructed, "and breathe through the third eye."

Andor inhaled deeply through the spot of pure light he imagined between his eyebrows, and his body slowly filled with sunlight—every corner of his being, every muscle, every blood vessel, every burning sinew.

His hands and his feet were on the ground while he was trying hard to keep his legs straight as well as his back. An agonizing exercise. He was stretched to the limit, but it felt good. The pain was healthy. Pleasant even.

There was only one thing that could make this moment even better.

He opened his eyes and glanced up to where the roundest arse in Midgard was stuck in the air. He could see her beautiful face upside down behind her long, straight legs, her eyes closed. The sight brought the most enjoyable memories to his mind. Last night, he had held that arse in his hands as Cathy rode his cock, her eyes closed in pure bliss. Forgetting the pain in the backs of his legs, he smiled. The tightness dissolved a little, and his legs stretched even further.

"Breathe," his wife said and looked straight at him. "Andor!"

"I am dealing with the discomfort as best as I can. It seems that the sight of your arse is the best cure."

Behind him, three men and five women, who were exercising as well, chuckled. Cathy suppressed a smile.

"You need to breathe," she said.

He wiggled his eyebrows. "I like my way better."

She rolled her eyes, but he knew he'd brought a smile to her face, and that made his day even brighter.

He breathed in the sweet air of the hillside meadow in the autumn morning, with a whiff of freshly cut wood from the village below. Cathy did a yoga routine every morning. And Andor had begun joining her, which had led to other people being curious and trying it. Cathy encouraged anyone who wanted to join. The view from here was spectacular: the fjord curving among the mountains, the freshly built village below. The great hall was finished, as well as several other houses, the granary, the storage buildings, the smithy and carpentry, and all the other buildings necessary to winter in Hvaldalen.

Today was the harvest festival. There were guests in Hvaldalen to celebrate the rebuilding of the village. Andor's friends and allies from Norway and even Viking Bretland, including the most important ones of all—Svana's parents.

Cathy continued the sun salutation routine, which brought Andor the connection with his inner self that he had come to value. There were no ghosts anymore within him. No closed doors. There was peace and quiet and love.

After the yoga routine, he was warm, sweaty, and happy.

Fridstein and the others thanked Cathy for the session, rolled their leather yoga mats and went down to the village.

Andor drew Cathy to himself, and she grimaced. "We're both sweaty."

She evaded his arms with a playful smile, making him growl.

"Ah well, then I better wash you," Andor said. "Although I think you are delicious when you're a little salty."

She took a step back. "Only if you can catch me."

With a squeal, she picked up her mat and the purse with clean clothes and ran down the path towards the fjord. There was an inlet, away from the village, where a small river flowed into the fjord. It was a favorite place for the people to do their Saturday bathing. Except, it was not a Saturday, and everyone kept away from there after yoga, knowing they might see the jarl and his wife enjoying a bath.

The beautiful wench was fast, on her long, strong legs, but he was faster. He caught her almost at the bottom of the hill and put her over his shoulder, laying one hand on her gorgeous behind and giving it a couple of soft, satisfying slaps.

"Not getting away from me," he said.

"Put me down, Andor!" she cried. "This is humiliating. I'm supposed to be a jarl's wife, and you are behaving as if I'm plunder."

"You are plunder." He came to the inlet and put her down. "I raided Northumbria, Mercia and Wessex, and came home with you. Now, off with these clothes."

"I can do that myself, you know."

"I know. But you are my plunder and I want to plunder you."

She smiled and shook her head in mock disapproval, but he could tell she enjoyed it. And anything she enjoyed, he was ready to do ten times over. He undressed her, marveling at her flawless, appetizing curves, his erection already ready and hungry for her. Then he undressed himself.

He lifted her in his arms and walked into the water. The chill stole his breath. Cathy squealed a little. He kissed her when they were in the water up to their shoulders, and his blood boiled in his veins from the sweet strokes of her tongue and the softness of her lips, and the chill disappeared. He could boil the water in the inlet with the heat he produced from touching her.

He had her—gently, sweetly—because he could not do otherwise. Because when their bodies were connected, and her delicious warmth enveloped him, it felt like home.

She was home.

When they were done and clean, they sat on the shore in clean clothes, wrapped in each other's arms, watching the mountains and the fjord. Water splashed gently against the rocky shore. The feast needed to be prepared, the guests needed to be entertained, and generally, the day promised to be busy, so Andor wanted to enjoy a few more moments of peace with Cathy, alone.

"I have something for you," Cathy said, excitement ringing in her voice.

Andor cocked his head to look at her profile—she sat in his arms, her back pressed against his torso, his arms around her waist.

"You do? What?"

She stood up and clasped his hands in hers. "I was waiting for a special moment to give these two things to you. Well, Fridstein helped to hide them. Without him, I'd probably have given in as one of them was finally ready."

Andor stood up, too. "You've already given me so much. Odin and Thor, I do not need anything more. You are with me. The village is being rebuilt. What else could I possibly want?"

"You will want *this*. And today, to celebrate our home, our first harvest festival, our first real bedroom...I think it is the right time."

Andor's brows crawled up. "What is it?"

She sank to the ground, reached behind some bushes, and removed her gift. She held it out to him with both hands. The object was long and straight and wrapped in linen.

"I lost Dragon's Trouble, and I know how important it was to you. Here."

He took the bundle from her hands, all sparks of humor that had been playing in his body gone. It was heavy. It was likely a sword—the weight felt right and familiar in his hands. With every layer of linen he unwrapped, the realization gripped his body like a closing fist. When the final layer fell away, a sword did, indeed, lay in his hands. From the very edge to the pommel, Andor studied it, not believing his eyes.

Dragon's Trouble, whole and shining like new, lay in his hands.

His throat clenched as he tried and failed to suppress the giant wave of love as gratitude washed over him. He studied the dragon on the iron pommel and every curve of the ornate patterns of fire on the cross guard. The iron looked polished, as though newly cast. The deer antler handle bound with silver cords still had scratches on it, but unlike metal, it was impossible to do anything about that.

The blade...

The blade was like new. Great steel, sharp, no scratches, no indents, no signs it was ever chipped.

Andor held Dragon's Trouble with both hands and cut through the air, then hit an invisible target from left, then right.

"Perfection." Andor looked at Cathy.

She watched him with tears in her eyes and a smile on her face.

Andor felt as if he suddenly did not have enough air to breathe. He remembered his wedding day with Svana, when she had given him the sword as her present. Her straight, proud back, her green eyes shining with pride and joy as he had tried the same movements. "There is no one in this world stronger or more honorable a warrior than you, my husband," she had said to him then. And his shoulders had straightened, his chin had lifted, knowing that his wife stood behind him.

She did now, too. Her blessing was in this sword. It was in the air. It was in every building that was being rebuilt. It was in his people.

And it was in Cathy, more than anything.

Andor's eyes prickled as he took in a deep breath. "How did you find it?" he asked.

"When I returned to this time, I landed in Wessex, at the same beach in Devon, which was exactly what I wanted because I was determined to find that sword. When I arrived at the Wilham monastery to ask if they knew anything about its whereabouts, Aethelred admitted they had hidden Dragon's Trouble."

Andor's mouth fell open. "They did? It was there the whole time?"

"Yes. They didn't want you to kill anyone. But I explained how much it meant to you and what had happened to Svana. Aethelred gave it back on one condition, that it would not be used on the Saxon territories against his countrymen."

Andor shook his head. "I wish you would not make promises like that for me, but for this sword, I think this is a condition I can honor."

"Good. I also left them a generous donation from the stuff I brought with me. They saved your life when they knew you were the enemy, and I wanted to thank them. I left them some medicine, surgical tools, and several medical books written in Latin that I bought at antique auctions before I left LA. Gold and silver weren't the only things I brought."

"Oh yes, my rich wife. You arrived prepared. But trust me, I can give you all the treasure your heart desires. You did not need to bring anything from your time. Though I am glad those riches bought your passage here to me, and I am pleased the monks have been repaid for their kindness—even if they did take my sword. But tell me one thing. Why did you not give it to me right away?"

"I wanted it to be repaired. When I reached York, the blacksmith who made the shield said that I could get the sword repaired here, that you have a good blacksmith. Otherwise, I'd have had to wait too long."

"The shield?" Andor frowned.

Cathy sighed. "Darn it. I spoiled the second present."

She rummaged in the bushes again, then protruded a beautiful shield.

"You have Svana's sword—she gave you the ability to attack and defend. I want to give you the ability to protect yourself. A shield."

Andor stood, speechless, watching her. Could the gods bless him even more than they already had? He regarded the shield. It was made of good quality oak, well held by an iron rim, with a strong iron boss in the middle. But the best feature of the shield was its face. There was a beautiful, ornate carving of waves going one into the other, and a woman, tall and strong—Cathy, he realized—standing on a strange board, knees bent like she was going into a yoga pose.

The waves played and flew and made foam, in an unending ornament.

"Is it the surf?" Andor said, his voice coarse from the emotion that tightened his throat.

Cathy beamed. "Yes! It is the surf. And this, what is shown here, is surfing, like I told you about. That was the thing Brad used to do. He was the best in the world."

Andor smiled and studied the pattern, imagining how someone could stand on such a board and ride a wave like that. Breathtaking. He wished he could see that.

"Another blessing. You and I have two people watching over us, Cathy."

Cathy smiled at him and her eyes filled with tears. "We do."

Andor took the shield in his hands. "I can see it was the work of a craftsman." He turned the shield around and looked at the back. "It's not too heavy, perfectly made, good grip, an appropriate length of the strap."

He put it over his shoulder, and it fit perfectly. Then he took it in his hand and assumed the protective position he would use when he would hide behind it while holding a sword over it.

"I ordered it from Völundr, the smith himself," Cathy said.

Andor stared at her, feeling his mouth open a little.

"No, I'm joking." Cathy laughed. "I ordered it while I was looking for a ship in York."

Andor chuckled and said, "The shield will serve me well, Cathy. Thank you. This is a perfect gift."

She blushed, clearly content with herself. "Now you have something from Svana, and you have something from me, too."

Andor laughed a little and continued studying it. "Shields rarely get one, but this one needs a name."

"The Surf?" Cathy said.

"The Surf of Time. A great name for a shield."

Cathy breathed out. "Oh, I'm so glad you like it, Andor. I

thought of the surf because of how we met. I traveled to you from the surf in Los Angeles to the surf in Devon—I mean, Wessex. And then here, too, by sea. From surf to surf—through time."

Love and happiness spread through Andor like a surge of waves. He put the shield aside and kissed her, forgetting all sense of time, space, shields, and everything else.

"What do you say we go to the bedroom and consummate our marriage," he whispered against her lips.

"Andor, we've already consummated our marriage countless times. You're stuck with me forever."

"I cannot let you go now without thanking you for the best present of my life. Except you coming back to me."

Cathy smiled and tears of joy misted her eyes. "Okay, let's consummate our marriage."

He laughed slightly and lifted her up so that her legs hugged his hips and he supported her arse with his arms.

"Hold on, my sweet," he said. "I am about to rock you on the highest surf of your life."

"There isn't any other kind with you, my Viking."

THANK you for reading VIKING'S CLAIM. I hope you loved Cathy and Andor's story. Find out what happens next when the Norns send Mia to meet her soulmate Hakon the Beast in VIKING'S BRIDE.

A MISTAKEN IDENTITY. A forced marriage. A secret baby. When a pregnant woman escapes to the past, will she find love and passion in a vengeful Viking's arms?

. . .

READ **VIKING'S BRIDE** now >
"WOW! I absolutely loved this story!"

SIGN-UP FOR MARIAH STONE'S Newsletter:
http://mariahstone.com/signup

FEELING LIKE A BILLION DOLLARS?

And the Norns are sending people to the future, too. If you haven't read Channing and Ella's story yet, be sure to pick up AGE OF WOLVES.

There's more to tattooed billionaire, Channing Hakonson, than detective Ella O'Conner could have ever imagined—something mystical and ancient.

READ **AGE OF WOLVES** now >
"Great twists and turns. I just couldn't stop reading!"

. . .

Or stay in the Viking Age and read an excerpt from VIKING'S BRIDE.

Boston, June 21, 2019

"Do you think it's a boy or a girl?" Mia's friend Carla asked, taking a sip of coffee from a paper cup.

Mia's fingers were warm where they touched the smooth black-and-white ultrasound picture. On it was a little human. The round form of the head, the perfect curve of the vertebrae, the five little fingers waving at her filled her heart with so much love, it was about to explode.

The smells assaulting her in the Massachusetts General Hospital cafeteria made Mia slightly nauseated. Coffee, for which she could kill; donuts; and a hint of bleach. Doctors and nurses in uniforms sat together having lunch, visitors hunkered down at separate tables—some chatting with friends and family, others staring tiredly into the distance. A couple of yuccas stood in the corners by the floor-to-ceiling windows. The cafeteria buzzed quietly with voices.

"I don't know." Mia touched the little hand on the ultrasound with her thumb and smiled. It was a boy. Somehow, she just knew. She didn't want to share the knowledge with anyone, as though it was an intimate secret between her and the baby.

Carla and Mia sat near the window. At the table behind Carla was an old lady in a salad-green suit. Her hair as white as snow, a cup of tea on the table, she was knitting, the needles in her hands jumping up and down like the lines of a vitals monitor. The lady stole a curious glance at Mia and the ultrasound picture in her hand. Mia's breath caught in her throat. How strange. Mia flashed a polite smile at the lady.

"A mafia boss's baby... Still can't believe it." Carla shook her head, then leaned closer and dropped her voice to a whisper. "I thought you wanted to break up with him."

Cold sweat ran down Mia's spine at the mention of her ex-boyfriend. "I left him."

"You did? When? Why didn't you tell me?"

"Three days ago. Three of the happiest days of my life."

Carla's eyes lay on the ultrasound. "But he doesn't know about the baby, does he?"

"No. Of course not."

"What would happen if he found out?"

Mia's stomach dropped. "He'd never let me go. You didn't tell your brother you saw me here, did you?" Mia glanced around. "I must be paranoid, but I still keep looking over my shoulder. I can't really believe Dan agreed it was over."

Carla laughed nervously. "I can't believe I introduced you two in the first place! To think, if it wasn't for him, you'd be a pediatrician now. We'd work here together."

Mia shuddered, and the sleeve of her long summer dress shifted enough to reveal the yellowing bruise on her forearm. She blushed and moved to cover it, but Carla noticed. Her eyes darted away, as if she had just seen something too private. Mia's cheeks burned.

"That's all right." Mia pursed her lips. "I'll never let a man treat me like that again. Tomorrow I'm starting a new life. No men. Just me and the baby. Away from Boston."

Carla frowned. "Are you leaving?"

"I got a job far from here, in the middle of nowhere. I can't finish my residency program yet, but someday I will. My new life starts tomorrow morning when I get on the plane."

Carla's eyebrows rose. "And you are telling me *now?*"

"I couldn't risk it."

As the words left her mouth, a shadow fell over the table, a tall figure silhouetted against the sun. His scent reached Mia's nostrils: elegant masculine cologne and the faintest acrid whiff of gun oil. Painful shivers ran across her whole body, and she moved her hand to hide the ultrasound under the table, but his heavy palm smacked the picture to the tabletop. His dry, warm skin burned her icy cold hand.

"Couldn't risk what?" His voice purred next to her ear, his breath stinging her cheek.

He released her hand and pulled on the ultrasound, but she clenched it so tight her fingernails whitened. He jerked it from her hand, cutting her finger. Blood smeared the edge of the image.

Mia jumped up, kicking her chair back, and all eyes shot to her. Her pulse beat in her temples, her chest hurt, and her legs turned to jelly. Outside, Dan's bodyguards, Romeo and Carl, stood waiting. Her stomach dropped.

Dan's eyes were intense as he took in every detail of the ultrasound. He was a handsome man, with short dark hair and large dark eyes with long and thick lashes. He had high cheekbones, and his square jaw was clean shaven. He wore one of his tailored charcoal Italian suits with a white shirt and no tie. He looked like a CEO or a law firm partner—the illusion that Mia had fallen for three years earlier, when they'd first met. She should have suspected something, silly her. No CEO or lawyer had the mountain of pure muscle Dan had acquired from daily combat training. The mistake had cost her everything.

He met her gaze, and a chill washed over her. "I can't believe. That you hid this. From me." His voice was like the distant roar of a truck.

Mia began shaking. "How did you find me?"

"Little bird told me you went to an ob-gyn, and I wanted to

make sure you were all right." He glanced at Carla.

Shock hit Mia like a train. "How could you, Carla?"

Carla looked away. "I'm so sorry, Mia! I had no idea you two split up! And I didn't tell *him*."

"You told Gabe?"

Carla nodded. Gabe was Carla's brother who worked for Dan.

Nausea rose in Mia's stomach again. She shouldn't think about it. Not now. She needed to deal with Dan. She took a cleansing breath, like every time she had dealt with his crazy temper. More collected, she met his dark gaze.

"We are over, remember?"

He laughed, then his face turned into an emotionless mask. "Not after this. You are carrying my child. Do you think I'm going to let it grow up in a broken home?"

"There is no home for him with you—"

"Him?" An emotion touched his eyes. "A boy?"

She cursed herself. Dan had always dreamed of having a son. "I'm not sure."

"But you think it's a boy."

"I don't know, Dan! What does it matter?"

"You're right. It doesn't. A boy or a girl, I won't let my child grow up with separated parents. This changes everything. You come back to me, we get married, and we work on our relationship. We'll go to a shrink."

Mia's lips trembled. "But you don't love me, Dan."

His eyes turned black. "You are wrong. I never stopped loving you, *bella*."

The words every woman craved to hear turned Mia's blood into ice. She shook her head. "We're over. No amount of counseling can fix us. Too much has happened. The women, your temper..."

She only needed to get him to let her go home. Hell, just let her go, period. She'd disappear.

"You're right, but you are making me a better man. I'm more in control since you have been in my life than ever before. I'll work on my temper, and there will be no more women. I'll make you see the man you once loved."

That was impossible. She *had* loved him until she'd learned the truth about his occupation—something he hadn't revealed until they'd moved in together. She raised her chin. "How will you make me feel anything for you? Will you beat me again?"

His nostrils flared, and the vein on his temple twitched. "Don't. If you want me to work on my temper, I'll work on my temper. I won't touch a hair on your head. Not like *that*." Then he added in a low voice, "I hated when I did that to you."

How many times had she heard that over the past two and a half years?

"I am *not* coming back."

He grabbed her hand and pulled her to his chest. "Yes, you are."

She struggled to free herself, useless of course. But making a scene could be her chance.

"Let me go or I'll scream," Mia spat.

"No, you won't, bella." Dan moved his arm, and through the thin silk of her dress, she felt the cold barrel of his gun.

Needles pricked her from head to toe. "You won't shoot the mother of your child!"

"I will if she brings the cops down on me."

Mia's gut twisted, her free hand shot to her belly and lay on it protectively. She scanned the cafeteria for help. People glanced at them with curiosity, probably assuming a troubled couple argued. Carla only looked into her cup like a naughty puppy. That old lady in the green suit stopped knitting and watched Mia with concern. But what could a grandma do against Dan and his two bodyguards?

"Help," Mia mouthed to her.

But the woman didn't even twitch.

Dan picked up Mia's purse, shoved it to her, then dragged Mia after him, towards the doors for cafeteria staff. They walked past a bathroom door that read Employees Only and carried on towards the emergency exit. Desperation burned Mia like a fever. She had been so close to escaping Dan, to giving her baby a better future, a normal life—not a life inside the mafia.

But she'd failed. Dan now had a reason to find her anywhere she went. He had connections, ways of locating her, of chaining her to him. She'd had a chance after he had finally agreed to end the toxic relationship that had eaten her up physically and emotionally.

But she'd blown it. She never should have met with Carla. If she'd only waited until tomorrow...

They'd turned the corner of the empty corridor when a voice echoed behind them.

"Wait!"

They stopped and turned around, hope making Mia dizzy. But it was only the old lady.

"What?" Dan barked.

She stopped in front of them, small and harmless, not a trace of fear in her eyes.

"Listen, sweetheart." She talked directly to Mia with an accent that resembled German. "I have a way for you to escape, but it is not an easy path. There is a man who needs you, and you need him—a Viking."

Dan chuckled. "What, a Minnesota Viking? What are you blabbering about?"

"Expect strange things." She did not stop looking at Mia. "You will not believe them to be possible, but they will be the truth."

Mia swallowed. She had no idea what the lady was talking about, but Dan's grip around her arm became stronger and began hurting her, and she started to worry about the woman's safety. "You need to go. Now," Mia said.

"Honey, you forgot something back at the table." The woman's hand went into her purse, and Dan pointed his gun at her. But the woman removed a golden object. Mia squinted. Something like a spindle, from fairy tales?

What a random thing. The old lady held out the spindle. "Take it, you forgot it."

This was crazy. An escape? A golden spindle? A Viking that needed her?

Dan's hand had already stretched out to the spindle.

But there was something so deadly serious in the old lady's face, and so much strength in her gaze, as if destiny itself looked into Mia's eyes. She slapped away Dan's arm and reached out to the spindle. The lady's eyes smiled at that.

What did Mia logically expect would happen? Nothing. Maybe the lady would tase Dan, or maybe she had pepper spray, or maybe she was a retired karate world champion.

Or maybe it was a mean joke.

In any case, Mia went with it. Once the spindle touched her hand, a buzzing vibration went through her, and her head spun for real. Nausea made her stomach heave. The world around her began evaporating. The last thing she saw was Dan's astonished face, his hands grabbing at thin air in the place where she had stood a moment ago, and joy filled her nonexistent body.

And then everything disappeared.

KEEP READING VIKING'S BRIDE.

YOUR BONUS: A GLIMPSE INTO VIKING'S BRIDE

CHAPTER 1

Boston, June 21, 2019

"Do you think it's a boy or a girl?" Mia's friend Carla asked, taking a sip of coffee from a paper cup.

Mia's fingers were warm where they touched the smooth black-and-white ultrasound picture. On it was a little human. The round form of the head, the perfect curve of the vertebrae, the five little fingers waving at her filled her heart with so much love, it was about to explode.

The smells assaulting her in the Massachusetts General Hospital cafeteria made Mia slightly nauseated. Coffee, for which she could kill; donuts; and a hint of bleach. Doctors and nurses in uniforms sat together having lunch, visitors hunkered down at separate tables—some chatting with friends and family, others staring tiredly into the distance. A couple of yuccas stood in the corners by the floor-to-ceiling windows. The cafeteria buzzed quietly with voices.

"I don't know." Mia touched the little hand on the ultrasound with her thumb and smiled. It was a boy. Somehow, she just knew. She didn't want to share the knowledge with anyone, as though it was an intimate secret between her and the baby.

Carla and Mia sat near the window. At the table behind Carla was an old lady in a salad-green suit. Her hair as white as snow, a cup of tea on the table, she was knitting, the needles in her hands jumping up and down like the lines of a vitals monitor. The lady stole a curious glance at Mia and the ultrasound picture in her hand. Mia's breath caught in her throat. How strange. Mia flashed a polite smile at the lady.

"A mafia boss's baby... Still can't believe it." Carla shook her head, then leaned closer and dropped her voice to a whisper. "I thought you wanted to break up with him."

Cold sweat ran down Mia's spine at the mention of her ex-boyfriend. "I left him."

"You did? When? Why didn't you tell me?"

"Three days ago. Three of the happiest days of my life."

Carla's eyes lay on the ultrasound. "But he doesn't know about the baby, does he?"

"No. Of course not."

"What would happen if he found out?"

Mia's stomach dropped. "He'd never let me go. You didn't tell your brother you saw me here, did you?" Mia glanced around. "I must be paranoid, but I still keep looking over my shoulder. I can't really believe Dan agreed it was over."

Carla laughed nervously. "I can't believe I introduced you two in the first place! To think, if it wasn't for him, you'd be a pediatrician now. We'd work here together."

Mia shuddered, and the sleeve of her long summer dress shifted enough to reveal the yellowing bruise on her forearm. She blushed and moved to cover it, but Carla noticed. Her eyes darted away, as if she had just seen something too private. Mia's cheeks burned.

"That's all right." Mia pursed her lips. "I'll never let a man treat me like that again. Tomorrow I'm starting a new life. No men. Just me and the baby. Away from Boston."

Carla frowned. "Are you leaving?"

"I got a job far from here, in the middle of nowhere. I can't finish my residency program yet, but someday I will. My new life starts tomorrow morning when I get on the plane."

Carla's eyebrows rose. "And you are telling me *now*?"

"I couldn't risk it."

As the words left her mouth, a shadow fell over the table, a tall figure silhouetted against the sun. His scent reached Mia's nostrils: elegant masculine cologne and the faintest acrid whiff of gun oil. Painful shivers ran across her whole body, and she moved her hand to hide the ultrasound under the table, but his heavy palm smacked the picture to the tabletop. His dry, warm skin burned her icy cold hand.

"Couldn't risk what?" His voice purred next to her ear, his breath stinging her cheek.

He released her hand and pulled on the ultrasound, but she clenched it so tight her fingernails whitened. He jerked it from her hand, cutting her finger. Blood smeared the edge of the image.

Mia jumped up, kicking her chair back, and all eyes shot to her. Her pulse beat in her temples, her chest hurt, and her legs turned to jelly. Outside, Dan's bodyguards, Romeo and Carl, stood waiting. Her stomach dropped.

Dan's eyes were intense as he took in every detail of the ultrasound. He was a handsome man, with short dark hair and large dark eyes with long and thick lashes. He had high cheekbones, and his square jaw was clean shaven. He wore one of his tailored charcoal Italian suits with a white shirt and no tie. He looked like a CEO or a law firm partner—the illusion that Mia had fallen for three years earlier, when they'd first met. She should have suspected something, silly her. No CEO or lawyer had the mountain of pure muscle Dan had acquired from daily combat training. The mistake had cost her everything.

He met her gaze, and a chill washed over her. "I can't believe. That you hid this. From me." His voice was like the distant roar of a truck.

Mia began shaking. "How did you find me?"

"Little bird told me you went to an ob-gyn, and I wanted to make sure you were all right." He glanced at Carla.

Shock hit Mia like a train. "How could you, Carla?"

Carla looked away. "I'm so sorry, Mia! I had no idea you two split up! And I didn't tell *him*."

"You told Gabe?"

Carla nodded. Gabe was Carla's brother who worked for Dan.

Nausea rose in Mia's stomach again. She shouldn't think about it. Not now. She needed to deal with Dan. She took a cleansing breath, like every time she had dealt with his crazy temper. More collected, she met his dark gaze.

"We are over, remember?"

He laughed, then his face turned into an emotionless mask. "Not after this. You are carrying my child. Do you think I'm going to let it grow up in a broken home?"

"There is no home for him with you—"

"Him?" An emotion touched his eyes. "A boy?"

She cursed herself. Dan had always dreamed of having a son. "I'm not sure."

"But you think it's a boy."

"I don't know, Dan! What does it matter?"

"You're right. It doesn't. A boy or a girl, I won't let my child grow up with separated parents. This changes everything. You come back to me, we get married, and we work on our relationship. We'll go to a shrink."

Mia's lips trembled. "But you don't love me, Dan."

His eyes turned black. "You are wrong. I never stopped loving you, *bella*."

The words every woman craved to hear turned Mia's blood into ice. She shook her head. "We're over. No amount of counseling can fix us. Too much has happened. The women, your temper..."

She only needed to get him to let her go home. Hell, just let her go, period. She'd disappear.

"You're right, but you are making me a better man. I'm more in control since you have been in my life than ever before. I'll work on my temper, and there will be no more women. I'll make you see the man you once loved."

That was impossible. She *had* loved him until she'd learned the truth about his occupation—something he hadn't revealed until they'd moved in together. She raised her chin. "How will you make me feel anything for you? Will you beat me again?"

His nostrils flared, and the vein on his temple twitched. "Don't. If you want me to work on my temper, I'll work on my temper. I won't touch a hair on your head. Not like *that*." Then he added in a low voice, "I hated when I did that to you."

How many times had she heard that over the past two and a half years?

"I am *not* coming back."

He grabbed her hand and pulled her to his chest. "Yes, you are."

She struggled to free herself, useless of course. But making a scene could be her chance.

"Let me go or I'll scream," Mia spat.

"No, you won't, bella." Dan moved his arm, and through the thin silk of her dress, she felt the cold barrel of his gun.

Needles pricked her from head to toe. "You won't shoot the mother of your child!"

"I will if she brings the cops down on me."

Mia's gut twisted, her free hand shot to her belly and lay on it protectively. She scanned the cafeteria for help. People glanced at them with curiosity, probably assuming a troubled couple argued. Carla only looked into her cup like a naughty puppy. That old lady in the green suit stopped knitting and watched Mia with concern. But what could a grandma do against Dan and his two bodyguards?

"Help," Mia mouthed to her.

But the woman didn't even twitch.

Dan picked up Mia's purse, shoved it to her, then dragged Mia after him, towards the doors for cafeteria staff. They walked past a bathroom door that read Employees Only and carried on towards the emergency exit. Desperation burned Mia like a fever. She had been so close to escaping Dan, to giving her baby a better future, a normal life—not a life inside the mafia.

But she'd failed. Dan now had a reason to find her anywhere she went. He had connections, ways of locating her, of chaining her to him. She'd had a chance after he had finally agreed to end the toxic relationship that had eaten her up physically and emotionally.

But she'd blown it. She never should have met with Carla. If she'd only waited until tomorrow...

They'd turned the corner of the empty corridor when a voice echoed behind them.

"Wait!"

They stopped and turned around, hope making Mia dizzy. But it was only the old lady.

"What?" Dan barked.

She stopped in front of them, small and harmless, not a trace of fear in her eyes.

"Listen, sweetheart." She talked directly to Mia with an accent that resembled German. "I have a way for you to escape, but it is not an easy path. There is a man who needs you, and you need him—a Viking."

Dan chuckled. "What, a Minnesota Viking? What are you blabbering about?"

"Expect strange things." She did not stop looking at Mia. "You will not believe them to be possible, but they will be the truth."

Mia swallowed. She had no idea what the lady was talking about, but Dan's grip around her arm became stronger and began hurting her, and she started to worry about the woman's safety. "You need to go. Now," Mia said.

"Honey, you forgot something back at the table." The woman's hand went into her purse, and Dan pointed his gun at her. But the woman removed a golden object. Mia squinted. Something like a spindle, from fairy tales?

What a random thing. The old lady held out the spindle. "Take it, you forgot it."

This was crazy. An escape? A golden spindle? A Viking that needed her?

Dan's hand had already stretched out to the spindle.

But there was something so deadly serious in the old lady's face, and so much strength in her gaze, as if destiny itself looked into Mia's eyes. She slapped away Dan's arm and reached out to the spindle. The lady's eyes smiled at that.

What did Mia logically expect would happen? Nothing. Maybe the lady would tase Dan, or maybe she had pepper spray, or maybe she was a retired karate world champion.

Or maybe it was a mean joke.

In any case, Mia went with it. Once the spindle touched her hand, a buzzing vibration went through her, and her head spun for real. Nausea made her stomach heave. The world around her began evaporating. The last thing she saw was Dan's astonished face, his hands grabbing at thin air in the place where she had stood a moment ago, and joy filled her nonexistent body.

And then everything disappeared.

Keep reading Viking's Bride.

ALSO BY MARIAH STONE

MARIAH'S TIME TRAVEL ROMANCE SERIES

- Called by a Highlander
- Called by a Viking
- Called by a Pirate
- Fated

MARIAH'S REGENCY ROMANCE SERIES

- Dukes and Secrets

VIEW ALL OF MARIAH'S BOOKS IN READING ORDER

Scan the QR code for the complete list of Mariah's ebooks,
paperbacks, and audiobooks in reading order.

GET A FREE MARIAH STONE BOOK!

Join Mariah's mailing list to be the first to know of new releases, free books, special prices, and other author giveaways.

freehistoricalromancebooks.com

ENJOY THE BOOK? YOU CAN MAKE A DIFFERENCE!

Please, leave your honest review for the book.

As much as I'd love to, I don't have financial capacity like New York publishers to run ads in the newspaper or put posters in subway.

But I have something much, much more powerful!

Committed and loyal readers.

If you enjoyed the book, I'd be so grateful if you could spend five minutes leaving a review on the book's **sales page.**

Thank you very much!

Note on Historical Accuracy

With the passage of time, certain details are lost and often debated. For example, the location of the battle between Odda, ealdorman of Somerset, and Viking leader Ubba remains unknown. According to some historians, the battle took place near Countisbury Hill in Devon, while others claim it was Cannington Hill in Somerset. Both of these locations lie in the area of the Bristol Channel, around forty miles from each other. While the exact location is unclear, I've used artistic license and chosen the location that made the most sense for this story.

Another mysterious place from the book is Wayland's Smithy, a neolithic barrow. Wayland is the modern way of pronouncing Old English name *Wēland*. In Old Norse, it's *Völundr*. Because Saxons were Germanic tribes, just like other Scandinavian people including Norwegians, Danes and Swedes, their gods were similar. In this case, Wayland was a skilled smith who married a Valkyrie but then was enslaved by a Danish King who forced Wayland to work for him. According to the legend, Wayland came up with a terrible revenge plan for the king and freed himself by using the tools he forged. It's a fascinating and a dark story, and I thought Wayland's smithy was a perfect representation of the fear of the locals. During the time of Viking invasions, the recently Christian Wessex, Northumbria and other kingdoms undoubtedly heard the echoes of their old, dark, pagan past when they saw Vikings.

Acknowledgments

This is my favorite part of writing the book. THANK YOU:

Laura Barth, my amazing editor, who is my Yoda—only tall and pretty (no offense to the green Yoda).

My husband and my son who support me and for whom I do this.

My loyal, wonderful readers and the best ARC team in the world.

My beta-reader Susan Braithwaite who always does more and who tells the truth in a helpful, humorous and supportive way.

My writer group that is helpful and supportive and charges me with creativity and strength.

About Mariah Stone

Mariah Stone is a bestselling author of time travel romance novels, including her popular Called by a Highlander series and her hot Viking, Pirate, and Regency novels. With nearly one million books sold, Mariah writes about strong modern-day women falling in love with their soulmates across time. Her books are available worldwide in multiple languages in e-book, print, and audio.

Subscribe to Mariah's newsletter for a free time travel book today at mariahstone.com/signup!

facebook.com/mariahstoneauthor

instagram.com/mariahstoneauthor

bookbub.com/authors/mariah-stone

pinterest.com/mariahstoneauthor

amazon.com/Mariah-Stone/e/B07JVW28PJ